BLEED THEM DRY

COURTNEY CLARK MICHAELS

To Elle, for letting me jump on board the vampire ship. I love you!

BEFORE YOU START READING

This is a dark romance with two morally complicated main characters. Please be aware of the following contents that may be triggering to readers:

- Capitalism
- The United States health care system
- Historic death of family members
- Absent parent
- Billionaires
- Mentions of drug abuse, including overdose
- Murder
- Suicide ideation
- Blood and gore
- Stalking
- Explicit intimate scenes
- Bloodsucking, both consensual and
- nonconsensual
- Knife violence
- Assault of an assailant

- Murder
- Mugging
- Accidental fire
- Intimate partner violence
- Resuscitation

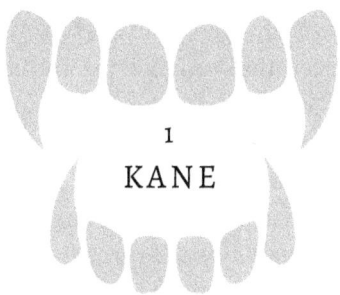

1

KANE

*E*verybody wonders what it would be like to kill someone.

I don't have to wonder. I know.

Sure, people have died in front of me. Dozens of times, starting with my mother when I was eight years old. But there's a difference between standing in a healer's hut or an operating theatre, watching life leave a body under the lights while machines beep and people rush around, and the whine-boom of the defibrillator echoes overhead, and the sad muffled sobs on the other end of the phone when you've handed down a death sentence.

Sometimes they scream instead.

I don't blame them.

This job fucking sucks. They pack us in like sardines, crammed inside gray cubicles, suffocating in artificial air and fluorescent light. A headset, a phone, constant chatter surrounding us. Not the back-and-forth banter of a team, the hushed tones of competition.

They do it on purpose.

There's no reason we can't reject health insurance claims

from the comfort of our own couches. But like the predators they're named for, the bigwigs of Apex City like us here, where they can watch over us in person. Watch us scrambling to meet targets that keep moving, inhaling stale oxygen and protein bars to sustain us long enough to escape the tight fist of capitalism for another day.

It hurts more today for some reason.

Maybe it's the moon, the way it hung low and full in the sky as I made my way to work through the milky twilight. Full moons always remind me of home, of my kuia.

She'd be ashamed of me.

I'm ashamed of me.

I came to this country to put my nursing degree to good use. Hell, to pay off some of the debt that came along with it. America might be a dystopian nightmare, but healthcare is a profitable skill to have in a social apocalypse.

Kuia was supportive enough of me leaving the island to train as a nurse on the mainland of Aotearoa New Zealand, even if she did think the old ways were better than anything scientific healthcare had come up with in the last century.

But this? Trapped in a call centre telling a sobbing woman she'd be a widow by the end of the year because her husband missed a payment on his health insurance policy eight months ago?

There's not enough native herbs on the island for her to cleanse me of my sins, even if she was still alive to bother.

"You good?" Bindi mutters beside me.

"Nope," I reply, jotting the relevant details into my client's case file.

She gives a little humph. Bindi's Australian, and I was raised on the island of Mākutu, off the coast of New Zealand. By the law of ex-pats, we're the closest thing to work friends you can get here.

"Going on break," I mutter. It's a risky move. There's no

fucking unions here to ensure I get time to piss and eat, that's for sure. But since I've just ruined Mrs. Talbot's life as she knows it, I could use a breather.

Sure enough, the supervisor Edgar is glaring at me as I unfold myself from my seat and shuffle towards the door. He can glare all he likes. He gets paid a shitload more than me for doing five-eighths of fuck all.

The chilly evening air wraps around me, nature in all her beauty surrounding me even here in a city halfway around the world. I welcome it, but not enough to resist a puff on my vape as I lean against the cinderblock wall of the alley.

For all that I was raised in nature, I'm a man who loves a bit of artifice. That's why I thought this city would suit me. And it did, for a bit. Slick people under sparkling skies, edged with the shine of synthetic substances that slid through my veins. I loved it all, and it loved me back.

Until it didn't.

Now I'm basically jobless, this shitty call centre the only thing between me and deportation. No friends – except Bindi maybe, if she's in the mood – no lovers, just a busted mattress in an apartment uptown with four other room-mates, above a dive bar that doesn't even discount our drinks.

I've still got eight months left on my visa, though, and I'm determined to make the most of them. Boys like me don't make it out of the South Pacific often, and when we do it's with the knowledge that we'll be back. The Bermuda triangle has nothing on Polynesia for sucking you in and keeping you there.

I should be grateful. There are worse places to live. But not a lot worse for a bisexual kid of indistinct heritage on a small island where everyone knows your fucking business. Aotearoa New Zealand was an escape, but not enough. I could still feel the island calling me, heralding me back.

So I ran further.

To this shitty alley, in this shitty city, in this shitty country, under the same godsdamned moon.

But I'm still the same person, which means when he comes for me, I'm ready.

My knife glints silver against the pale skin of his neck, and he stares me down, gnashing his teeth in obvious frustration that the element of surprise has just switched hands.

"You better fuck off," I warn him. "I'm not the one you want to test tonight."

The stranger tilts his head slightly, studying me. An icy shiver runs down my spine but I ignore it, focusing instead on my knife, on keeping it lodged against the thick column of his throat.

"Kanu?"

He knows my name. My real name. My shock must be evident on my face, because the stranger smiles, a sly twist of his lips that reveals a pair of pointed canines.

"On the contrary," he purrs. "You're exactly the one I want. I've been searching for you for a very long time."

Fuck.

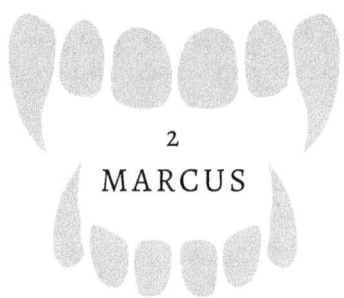

2
MARCUS

*T*he boy surprises me.

Rare, that. Surprises don't come easy when you've lived almost a quarter of a millennium.

But aside from a pleasant twang at the back of my mind, I refuse to acknowledge it. I won't be dissuaded from my mission, not now that I'm so close to completion.

"I've been searching for you for a very long time," I tell him, unable to stop the spread of triumph across my face. Why should I? I'm days – hours, maybe – from success.

There's a flicker in his eyes – they're gray, which makes him an anomaly where he comes from. In fact, he looks almost nothing like the usual inhabitants of the island. He's tanned, but not dark, tall, slim, the kind of body that always seems to move in an unhurried rhythm. Even now, strange eyes hard and his knife biting at my throat, there's a looseness to him.

Either he doesn't realise who I am, or he's got no concerns about his ability to slay me.

Both, perhaps. Or neither. Perhaps he suspects I'm one of the derelict that roam these streets, spouting nonsense.

Well, I know better than others that one society's nonsense is another's way of life. After all, my own arrogance about the practices of others has brought me here, to the filthy streets of this city, in a land I'd vowed never to set foot on again.

But needs must, and I need Kanu.

"Sorry to disappoint," the boy in question drawls. "But if you're looking for a fuck, I'm busy tonight. Try the Crimson District."

"I'm not interested in fucking you." My dick twitches as I say it. Huh. Interesting. I file that away to examine later. When my esophagus isn't in immediate danger of being sliced open. "Put your knife away and let me buy you a drink."

"That's what all the men who want to fuck me say."

I give him a reproachful look, and he grins back cockily. He can't be more than thirty in human years, but the casual tone to his voice makes him seem younger.

He's young enough. I'd prefer to have someone a little more experienced rip my soul from my body, but blood cannot be denied.

We are bound by it, he and I.

"I wish to speak with you. Somewhere private."

"What's more private than a creepy alley?"

As if by divine fate, a couple stumble into the alley's mouth, their laughter bouncing off the cinderblock.

In a flash, Kanu's blade disappears and he's leaning against the wall exhaling a long plume of smoke from his nostrils, the picture of innocence.

His smoke smells like marzipan, and I'm hit with a sudden memory of my mother's parlour – of the way the stiff silk of her dress brushed against my knee as she sat beside me and offered me sweet morsels while my sister's pianoforte pinged merrily in the background.

"Oh!" One of the amorous couple straightens suddenly, eyes on us. He's tipsy. I can smell his blood from here, but the rye is light, an accent to the rich flavor that pulses through his veins. It'd be just enough to warm my throat.

My mouth waters.

"Evening, friend." Kanu offers the other man an irreverent salute. Surely he can't have a military background? Not with that weak wrist action and a mess of dirty blond hair that falls to his collarbone.

The man nods stiffly, all evidence of his good humor gone. "Come on, Hailey. Let's get going."

"You alright, Hailey?" My saviour's stance is relaxed, but the arch of his brow alerts me to the genuine question beneath the casual inquiry.

"Fine, thanks," she mumbles. Her eyes dart between Kanu and I, as though we are the ones she should be wary of, and not the lover who lurks behind her with liquor on his lips.

Statistics don't lie, but she is a smart girl, Hailey. She recognises the danger the two of us pose, without knowing how or why her instincts prickle. She is even smarter for her choice of beverage tonight. Her blood is tainted with moscato. I am not tempted in the slightest.

The couple back out of the alley and continue on their way, footsteps hurrying on asphalt.

Kanu and I turn to face each other again. His knife remains hidden but I keep my distance. Not that I fear him – I could overpower him in an instant, whatever gifts he's inherited from his ancestors. But I'm here to seek assistance, not to antagonise. Even if he does look delicious.

"Kanu–"

"Kane," he interrupts. "I go by Kane here."

I nod. "Kane, then. I have an urgent matter that requires your attention."

He exhales another plume of marzipan smoke. "I'm not interested."

"It's not a question of your interest."

He shrugs. "I don't do shit that doesn't interest me."

I gesture to the building behind him. "Like that?"

"They pay me."

"I can pay you."

That interests him. I see it in his eyes, even as he tempers his expression to cover it.

"I have to get back in."

He doesn't. His services are priceless to me, I'll pay anything to procure them. "I'll wait in the lobby."

He eyes my mouth with one brow raised. "You will?"

Mercy be, does the man know nothing of my kind and our ways? For the first time since I began this quest unease stirs in my gut.

"I will."

"I've got another five hours to go."

"I'll wait."

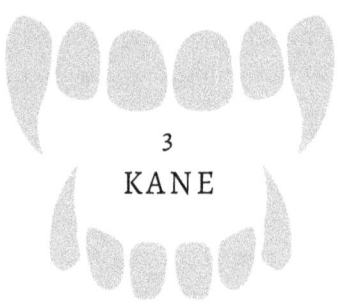

3

KANE

*T*here's a vampire in the lobby.
Waiting for me.

It's not the way I expected tonight to go, but honestly nothing about my time in Apex City has gone to plan. First there was my nursing career, cut short in a round of layoffs made under the guise of economic downturn, as if life or death gives a fuck about the profit margins of privatised healthcare. Then my relationship – the stars in Bethany's eyes faded real quick when she realised I liked to fuck dudes as well, no matter how monogamous I'd been while we were together. Liked to think she was progressive, Bethany did, but her long-lost faith sprang to life like Jesus himself on the heels of my revelation, and I was out in the cold. Literally, since we'd been living together. The roommate situation I'm in now isn't ideal either, but it's nothing compared to the clusterfuck of having an undead stalker flipping through a back issue of *People* and waiting for me to finish processing insurance claims.

I suppose it makes sense. This job's been sucking the life

out of me so it has a head start, but no doubt Count Hotula has come calling to finish the job.

Bloodlust is one thing. But slayer blood? Doesn't matter how diluted it is – how diluted *I* am thanks to my questionable paternal donor – it's still going to have the other boogeymen dying for a Kane-shaped kegstand.

Couple that with the witch-shit and I'm the Dom Perignon of hemoglobins. The hottest drink in town.

"Oi!"

Bindi's voice snaps me out of the fog. "What?"

"I'm going to get breakfast. You want to come?"

I *do* want to get breakfast with Bindi. She's got amazing taste in diners and is cool with letting me finish her leftovers. Extra food is extra food and in this economy that can only be a good thing.

"I can't," I grimace. "Got a meeting." With death. His, preferably.

Bindi shrugs. "Suit yourself. See you tomorrow."

I bloody hope so.

She wanders away, backpack slung over one shoulder, giving Edgar the finger when he's not looking. She slips through the door to the office as all the other poor souls line up to trail in and take our places, the day shift of dream destruction here to fuck up more people's lives.

It's not that I don't believe in health insurance. Admittedly that's easy to say given Mākutu is an territory of Aotearoa New Zealand, and free or subsidized medical treatment is pretty easy to come by. But health insurance has its place. It's *this* I hate – the tricky policy wording, the poison-tipped darts hidden in the fine print that mean more often than not the big companies who've spent years bleeding their clients in premiums turn around and deny treatment on a technicality.

I got into healthcare because I wanted to help people. But

all I'm surrounded by these days is suffering.

That's the price everyone's willing to pay for the American Dream, I guess. No green light here, just the red blink of endless calls seeking help and getting no response.

Heaving a sigh, I get to my feet, Jose from the day shift slipping right into it before I've even got my headset off.

"Good luck," I tell him but he just grunts in return, his finger already hovering over the lit button.

True to his word, the vampire is still in the lobby. His fingers are steepled together, one ankle resting on the opposite knee, head tilted back and eyes closed. He looks like a finance bro practicing meditation, and I've seen enough of those to recognise that I want nothing to do with him for reasons undead or otherwise.

Gods Almighty, he's hot. Dark hair, chiseled jaw, straight nose, thick brows. The kind of traditional good-looking white man you could photograph in sepia tones and have no idea what decade you were in, save the clothes.

If you photographed him without clothes... well, that'd be something else all together.

"I want coffee," I announce. "And breakfast." I'm bitter about missing out on Bindi's invitation.

"Anything you like," he drawls, cracking one eye open. They're brown, the kind that shine gold in the right light. I didn't notice earlier because being distracted by eye colour when you've got your knife to someone's throat is how you end up dead.

Or alternatively, how you end up having the blood sucked out of you by a creature of the night.

Speaking of...

"You gonna be alright out there?" I nod towards the plate glass windows of the lobby. The street outside is just visible as the morning paints it navy blue. Dawn's almost here. "I can just take your credit card and buy my own shit if you need to cower here until nightfall."

A plane ticket maybe. Definitely a muffin.

The vampire does not find this amusing. "I am not bothered by sunlight."

Huh. New information.

Is it new though? Is this something Kuia taught me in my youth that gear and grass have wiped from my memory? Denial might be the river that kept me running but a lot of other shit polluted that water on the way here.

"Good to know," I say lightly instead. "Come on then, Moneybags. You're buying."

He unfolds himself from the chair with an effortless kind of grace. "Marcus."

"What's that, mate?"

"My name is Marcus."

"Mate, if I wanted to know my murderer's name I'd wander up to one of those ICE cunts and introduce myself. I don't give a fuck what you call yourself."

"My name," he intones slowly, eyes intent on mine, "is Marcus Grosvenor. And I have no intention of murdering you."

"That's what they all say."

"Who?"

"Vampires."

He cocks his head like he's considering that. "Have you met many?"

"Nah."

"Pity," Marcus Growabeard or whatever muses. "You might wish for more experience by the time we're finished."

My stomach rumbles. It's been a long time since the package of microwave rice and soy sauce I scarfed down for dinner.

"We're finished as soon as breakfast is done," I tell him. "And you're paying."

A slight incline of his head. "Of course."

I don't trust him. But I fight better when I'm fed, so as long as he keeps his fangs to himself until I've had time to smash an omelette or something, we should be right.

I gesture for him to walk ahead of me. The wry look he gives me indicates he knows exactly what I'm doing but I'm not trying to be subtle. I learnt at an early age that politeness could get me killed, just for who I am. That's not even accounting for apex predator folklore shit. Doesn't stop me checking out his arse as he pushes through the revolving glass door onto the street though. I'm not dead yet, and the back of this man is as much a work of art as the front.

"Stop staring at my backside."

"Why?"

"It's distracting."

"Good. Distractions make you sloppy."

He pauses for a split second, his easy gait hitching before carrying on as if nothing has happened. "You don't find my backside distracting, then?"

I shrug, pulling my eye away and moving up so we're almost side to side. I hang slightly behind still. "It's a nice arse. Not nice enough to die for, but pretty good."

An exasperated huff. "I've told you I'm not going to hurt you."

I snort. "And yet you're one of a very long line of beautiful people to peddle me that exact line, so forgive me if I'm not interested in empty promises."

He stops then, properly, and I have to spin to stop from giving him my back. "I don't say things I don't mean." His expression is fierce, those brown eyes almost glowing as dawn cracks through the night in golden shafts.

"Moneybags–"

"Marcus."

"Marcus." I pat his shoulder. Gods, it feels like marble. Dude is *jacked*. "You're immortal. How can your promises mean anything if nobody around you lives long enough for you to honor them?"

Consternation crosses his face along with a flash of concern. Maybe I've stunned him with my Suduko-level philosophy, but it doesn't matter because a few feet away is the hotel I've been leading from the back towards.

"In there," I jerk my chin towards the door. "Let's get a table and you can have your crisis with a coffee like the living do."

He doesn't answer, but when I risk my neck and head inside first, he follows like a meek little lamb.

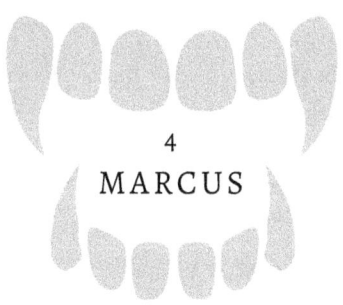

4

MARCUS

I've made a grave error.

This man thinks I'm immortal.

Before that, he questioned my tolerance to sunlight.

Earlier still, he assumed I couldn't enter a public building.

Fuck me dead.

My fate rests in the hands of a himbo.

I sit at the table in the hotel restaurant, marinating on this fact as Kanu – Kane – orders enough food to feed six men.

"You want anything?"

I pull my gaze from the white linen tablecloth. Kane and the server are both staring at me expectantly.

"I–" my voice sticks in my throat, and I swallow, clearing it loudly. "A pot of tea, thank you. English Breakfast."

"Certainly." The server disappears exactly the way servers should. I'd be impressed if I weren't choking on my panic.

"What do you know of my kind?"

The beautiful manchild raises a light eyebrow. "You're supposed to be a fairytale."

"But you know better."

He raises his water glass to his lips. "But I know better."

He swallows the clear liquid down and I watch his throat work, the play of muscles and veins under tanned skin.

"Who taught you?"

His eyes slide sideways. "My kuia." *His grandmother.* The language of the island still prickles over my skin after all this time.

"I'm sorry for your loss."

"Are you?" He replies cooly, gray eyes meeting mine. "She died suddenly. A year ago. How long did you say you'd been looking for me?"

A chuckle works its way out past the concern lodged in my throat. "Believe me, Kanu, if your grandmother were still alive, my journey would have ended with her. Her untimely passing is as unfortunate for me as for the rest of your family."

"It's Kane. So you were looking for her first?"

"I was looking for anyone still alive from the Tauhoe line."

There's a pause while our server returns with drinks. Kanu – Kane – tips half a jar of sugar into his milky coffee and stirs it loudly, the clack of silverware on china rattling through the air.

"You're not going to drink that?" He nods at the floral teapot by my elbow.

"It requires more time to steep. Some things can only be achieved through patience."

"Right." He quirks that damned eyebrow again. He really is a beautiful man. My cock makes its presence known once more as our gazes hold, and of all the times for my libido to resurface during this accursed hunt for answers, this is the worst possible moment.

The worst possible person.

"What have you been patient for, Marcus?" His voice is lower now, rasping across the table to me, gripping my balls and pulling tight. There's no doubt that he and I are feeling the same way – the sizzle of sexual attraction winding around us, binding us together in a doomed game of cat and mouse.

No matter the promise of pleasure, in the end there will only be one winner.

That's always been the plan, regardless of this inconvenient rope of lust twisting around me, the siren whisper in my ear — *have him, keep him, turn him.*

Men who listen to sirens do not fare well. I push the tempting chant of what I want aside and tell him instead what I need.

"I need you to kill me."

His eyes widen slightly. He's very good at appearing unfazed, this future murderer of mine, but I have the advantage of time on my side. Studying humans was a passion of mine for a couple of decades. It lost its charm somewhat after the realisation that they don't change too much, and certainly after the widespread adoption of Freud's psychoanalytic theories – the crackpot that he was. But reading the expression on someone's face is child's play for me. Before I was turned I was a regular cardshark at The Savile Club, and the art of practice has led to near-perfection. I don't need any of Freud's twattish students to concur that much of my distaste for the United States can be traced back to my poor treatment in Las Vegas in the middle of last century.

A prickish town, if ever there was one. Kane would probably adore it.

"Have you ever been to Las Vegas?"

"What?" He sounds distracted. "Yeah, for my thirtieth last year. Circle back to the killing part, would ya?"

"You enjoyed it." It's a statement not a question. Of course he did. He's the kind of man who would fit in perfectly with the glitter and glitz that covers up the streets of a grimy town. Even here in the filth of Apex City, he shimmers. It's as though he sucks the energy from the streets itself, turning it golden through sheer personality.

I myself have never had the talent of casual stardom. Perhaps why I was such an easy mark for my sire.

There's a flash of pain, swiping across my brain in a crimson mist. I do not like to think of my sire. When I think of the monster who made me, I am by the very bond of blood forced to think about *him*.

The monster *I* made.

I'll do anything to avoid that.

Including organising my own death at the hand of the beautiful man before me.

"Yeah, it was a good time. Lost some money and some dignity, but whatever right? That's life. Stay on track, old-timer."

"I am on track." Little does he know that every track I've taken in the last decade has led me here.

"Yeah? Just casually ordering your own suicide over a spot of tea?"

It takes everything I have not to roll my eyes. "If I could commit suicide, I would not need you. Your very involvement indicates that this surpasses such an easy exit."

Kane opens his mouth, but closes it again and leans back as his breakfast appears. Plate after plate, piled high with food.

"You cannot seriously eat all of that."

"I'm a growing boy." He runs a large hand over his stomach, and even through the cotton of his gray T-shirt I can see the outline of his abdominal muscles. This is a man who either spends hours torturing himself in one of those shiny exercise chambers, or this food will feed him for a week.

Given the light in his eyes when I offered him money for helping me, I suspect it is the latter.

"Excuse me," I say to the server as they place the final dish on the table. "I've changed my mind. May I please get a dozen scones? To go."

"Indeed."

"Last meal?" Kane asks around a mouthful of eggs.

"For you," I respond. "Scones freeze well. You'll be able to have them for breakfast next week."

He stops chewing. "You're buying me breakfast?"

"I thought that was clear." I indicate the spread before us.

"Next week's breakfasts?"

"Yes."

"As a 'thank you for murdering me' gift?"

"If you like." Honestly, I'm more concerned that the man might try to survive on that terrible concoction of sugar-laden milk he's been swigging since we arrived in lieu of proper nutrition.

"You're a weird guy, Marcus," Kane declares. "I like it. Now tell me why you want me to off you."

Warmth blooms in my stomach at his casual admission of affection. I'm positive it's connected to my ability to fill his freezer with baked goods rather than any personal qualities I might have, but after years without real companionship, any kind of acknowledgement seems a foreign delight.

"I have never been comfortable with my position," I begin carefully. This explanation requires some delicacy, and I've had plenty of time to plan for it. But I never counted on Kane.

"Your position as an undead citizen of the night?"

"Er, yes. Quite."

"Bummer. How'd it happen?"

The visions come again, crowding my mind with violent shrieks and the twisted memory of ripping skin, the copper tang against my tongue, pain exploding from behind my eyes.

"My turning was not a peaceful one. It was violent and

unexpected. I believe that my sire's intention was not to turn me, but rather to feed and leave me for dead. I fought back and in the battle I bit him enough to draw blood. Only a little, but it appears it was enough. I awoke three days later in the shadows of a bridge by the Thames. There was no sign of my sire, and it took little time to realise what had happened. Our society was not so far as yours is from the folklore, and stories of vampyre had been told to us as children by nurses wishing to scare us into silence at bedtimes."

"You go on a murder spree?"

I shut my eyes, wishing away the toxicity of this necessary reveal. "Yes."

"Dick. What happened then?"

"Intially, I sought power. I had been raised an aristocrat's son, and I was used to certain privileges. Looking back, my arrogance was extreme. With little knowledge of my own kind and a certainty that I needed to leave the land of my own family to spare them my ire, I took a ship to the antipodes."

"Naturally," Kane nods. "Nothing rich white dudes liked more back then than jumping a ship to the antipodes. Top-notch hobby, colonisation."

My mouth twists reluctantly. He isn't incorrect, but hearing my own history referred to with such sarcastic distaste highlights its absurdity. "It was my intention to colonise an island. Declare myself ruler and form a vamprye community of sorts."

"An army. You wanted a vampire army."

I shrug. "Perhaps. I wanted power, certainly. Status. But also people like me. Dead or alive, it didn't much matter, as long as they served me and provided me with entertainment. I had an active social life while living, and I saw no reason for my untimely death to interfere in that."

Kane mutters *"Thieving thundercunt"* under his voice so

softly I'm sure he didn't mean for me to hear. No matter. I have been called worse. Though not in such a robust accent for many years.

"Indeed," I agree, and pink steals across his cheeks. Adorable. "And the island I chose for my colony was Mākutu."

"How did my ancestors take that?"

"Not well," I admitted. "I had not prepared for such a forceful rejection of my plan. Nor for the magick they possessed."

"They fuck you up?" There's a thread of pride in his tone.

"Quite. In fact, they cursed me."

"Nice," he cackles, reaching for a stack of pancakes. "Constant itching like your body's coasted in stinging nettle? Unquenchable thirst? Make your willy fall off?"

"They cursed me with a soul."

He pauses, a forkful of pancakes halfway towards his lips. "A soul? That's all?"

"It is the heaviest burden I have ever carried," I inform him. "Although, I did not realise magickal castration was an option. That also would have been deeply problematic."

"What makes a soul the shittiest thing my whakapaka could hit you with?"

I pause, considering my words carefully. "When one has no soul, one does not comprehend the scale of pain they have caused. My early years as a vampyre were... messy. I was not in control of myself, nor did I care to be. An amplification, if you will, of the conscience my class lacked when it came to others combined with the ability to simply dispose of people who displeased me." I meet his eyes, serious now for the first time since he held a blade to my neck. "I was not a good man, before or after my turning. Your ancestors made sure they cursed me with the never-ending knowledge of that. I cannot go anywhere, see anyone, without being reminded of a different place, a different person, who reminds me of my past misdeeds."

"So you're feeling guilty and you wanna top yourself. Why not stop at the jewelry store for a nice silver chain, head to the beach, and chuck yourself on a bonfire in the middle of a sunny day?"

"I have. It was not effective. It would seem," I say slowly, "that until the curse itself is lifted, I am immune to the usual methods of self-harm my kind can utilise to end their lives."

"And you want me to break the curse." Kane sits back in his chair, a piece of sourdough toast clasped between blunt fingers tipped with navy blue nails.

"It's a blood curse," I acknowledge. "Everything I've learned indicates that it can only be broken by one who shares the blood of the witch who originally cursed me. Your great-great-great-great-great-grandmother."

"Kuia could have done it." He says it to himself, but I nod.

"Yes. Or your mother, were either of them still here. But they are not. You, Kanu Tauhoe, are my last chance at the final death."

He nods his head slowly, golden hair catching the light like a halo. My angel of death.

"Okay, then. Let's kill you."

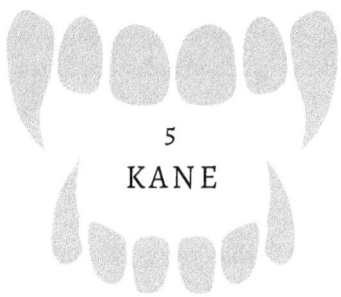

5

KANE

I haven't set foot in an occult shop since I've been on U.S. soil, but the instant I step through the door of the store on 23rd Street I'm hit with a wave of nostalgia so strong it almost brings me to my knees.

There's subtle differences to the scent of home. The blend of rongoā rakāu isn't quite right – no mānuka, no kawakawa, a noticeable dearth of horopito – but the sage is there, wrapping around the store like a warm hug. Its embrace highlights all the other elements – the rosemary for protection, the basil for love. There's crystals and candles everywhere, books and amulets. Boxes of incense line the shelves, but behind the everyday wiccan, there's real magic here.

I can feel it.

My own unfurls slowly, a muscle tight from disuse. It's been so long since I connected with this side of mine – longer than since I left Aotearoa New Zealand, since I left the island even. A decade, slightly more if I'm honest. The mainland universities paid lip service to rongoā, but in the battle between traditional indigenous medicine and the kind defined by the colonizers, only one ever showed up on my nursing exams. In the end, miles from my kuia, my whenua and my tāngata, rongoā slowly ended up pushed down under layers of book learning and eventual practice.

Something in Contreras Curiosities is awakening it.

Marcus follows me in after ushering me through the door first. I'm less concerned about giving him my back now that I know that he sought me out for assisted suicide. Right-wing wankers might claim that offing a dude goes against the Hippocratic oath, but I'm pretty sure it doesn't count if he's already dead. I'm more sure that I don't care what right-wing wankers think anyway. Besides, you see enough suffering and euthanasia starts to look like the more humane option.

There's a commotion at the store desk – a man crumples to the ground and two women rush to assist, one dropping a box of merchandise in her haste.

Shit. I move towards them, but I'm shoved out of the way by Marcus who moves at super-speed, pulling the struggling man to his feet and into a passionate embrace.

What the fuck?

"You saved my life," the dark haired stranger croaks, and I'm slightly mollified. "Do you remember me?"

"Of course I remember you." Marcus replies, his voice thick with emotion. "I could never forget you. I'm… My name is Marcus. Look at you. Are you all right?"

The apparently unforgettable stranger in Marcus's arms opens his mouth to answer, but doesn't get the chance. A massive hardcover book bounces off Marcus's skull instead, falling to the wooden floorboards with a resounding thunk.

"You fucking deadbeat!" the woman behind the counter snarls, her older counterpart moving hurriedly behind me to lock the door. The younger woman's fangs flash, eyes red, and I palm my knife discreetly.

"You just turned someone into a goddamn vampire and

just left him?" The younger woman fumes. "With a blood sample and a sticky note? What kind of irresponsible, reckless, inconsiderate, degenerate — "

"All right, all right!" Marcus is not thrilled about the descriptors being thrown around. His eyes are narrowed, full lips downturned. "Let's all just calm down and have a talk like rational immortals."

The woman still looks like she wants to murder him. *Go ahead babes, save me a job.*

Even as I think it, my stomach swoops and I rub my temple, trying to soothe my sudden headache.

"Where have you been?" the swooning man asks Marcus, gazing up at him with worshipful adoration. "Who are you? Where did you come from?"

Marcus looks around the shop, catching my eye and shrugging. The two of them make their way over to one of the plush armchairs in the corner and I hear him say "Well, I don't even know where to start. Maybe in 1880..."

"Your friend's an ass," the vampire girl says at my elbow.

"Mine?" I scoff. "What about your mate? Dropping to his knees like Aldis Hodge just walked in here with dick out."

"That's his sire," she hisses, fangs on full display. "Who turned him and bolted in the night, never to be seen again. Bash has been on his own since day one of his vampire life."

"Huh," I study the pair in the corner again. Abandon Daddy isn't the title I'd have picked for Marcus, but the woman seems sure and there's an undeniable cosy little tableau over in the corner there.

What do you know? my mind taunts me. *You've known him less than a day.*

"Who are you? You're not a vampire."

"Witch," I answer absently. It's been a while since I've used the term as an identifier, but I'm standing in an occult shop waiting for my vampire stalker to finish chatting with his undead baby so we can murder the former with magic. Now is no time to cosplay normal. I keep the slayer shit to myself though. There's a good chance vampires are touchy about a whole industry dedicated to killing them.

"What's your name, witch?"

"Kane. What's yours?"

"Mira. That's Bash."

"*Bash?*" I can't hide my incredulity and she scowls at me.

"It's short for Sebastian."

"Nice to meet you."

"You too, I guess."

We watch Marcus and Bash for a couple of minutes, then the older lady who disappeared once the fangs started flashing reappears from the back room with a tea tray.

"Cup of tea, lovelies?"

"Thanks, Fi." Mira grabs a cup and sucks the hot liquid down. I take an experimental sniff but all I can smell is chamomile and…

"Brandy?"

Fi shrugs. "Seemed appropriate."

Fuckin' A, Fi. I down it in one go.

"This is unexpected," Fi says brightly. "Sebastian was certain he'd never find his sire. How long has Marcus been in Apex City?"

I shrug. "I dunno. Only met him last night."

"Hmmm." She narrows her eyes at me. "And what is your relationship?"

"I'm supposed to murder him for money." Technically, I should do it for free but the slayers who wrote the old lore didn't have rent to pay.

Fi hitches an eyebrow. "Seems to be a lot of money in murder these days."

Mira snorts beside me.

"Well, needs must, I 'spose," I answer with false cheeriness. "Have you got anything that'll help?"

Fi leads me to the back room where the good shit is and I spend an hour or so leafing through books and Googling ingredients on my phone in an attempt to revise my traditional knowledge. I call my cousin Arihi as well, and leave a voicemail when she doesn't pick up.

"Kia ora. It's Kanu. Did Kuia ever mention a vampire coloniser the ancestors cursed a hundred plus years ago? Let me know ASAP. Hi to auntie. Mā te wā."

That should ensure she gets back to me pretty quick once she's finished checking out all the guests at the hotel she owns in the island's single town. If only to check I'm not back on the gear.

I eventually haul a couple of books out to the front counter where Fi looks them over carefully.

"Are you sure you know what you're doing, mijo?"

"Nope. But I've found that confidence usually gets me pretty far."

She doesn't find this amusing, instead pinning me with a serious gaze that slams into my gut. She reminds me of my kuia in this moment, somber eyes staring past the indifferent personality I've curated for myself over the years to compensate for the fear that tracks my every step. Fear of never being good enough, smart enough, kind enough. Fear of being too much, as well. Nurses get free therapy in Aotearoa New Zealand, so I'm a couple of years behind in appointments but not enough to unlearn that I'm a full fucking mess inside. Certainly not enough to learn how to unmask the authentic bits of myself without others' rejection swallowing me whole. Even the recent situation with Bethany made that perfectly clear. If my sexuality is enough to turn people away from me, what would they do when they uncover the whole clusterfuck I keep cloaked in the shroud of a Good Time Guy™?

"Confidence has its place in magic, but it's no substitute for the real thing," Fi murmurs and I lock my grin into place, jaw tightening, desperate for her to stop looking at me like that and just give me my books.

Fortunately, Mira pops up. "Bash isn't going to be happy you're offing his father."

"Sounds like something Bash needs to take up with Marcus then. I'm here for the money."

She looks me over carefully, considering. Her gaze doesn't go as deep as her aunt's, it's more calculated. I like that. I like people who are brazen about what they want, and what they can offer. Keeps things simple.

"There's a way to make money without killing Marcus."

"I have a job."

"Me too. Do you like yours?"

No. I hate it. I shake my head.

"Let me know if you need an alternative. Marcus has skills that could prove very beneficial."

"Crime doesn't pay, Mira," I give my voice a white-woman ring of disapproval and she laughs, a darkly satisfied chuckle that runs up my spine.

"On the contrary, Kane. Crime pays very well."

I give her a sour look. Not because I'm judging her, but because of the implication I'd let Marcus be my sugar daddy. I would, obviously, but I've just met the man. I have to pretend to have some pride.

Marcus and Bash make their way over to the counter, preventing me from having to answer, and Fi rings up my purchases, which Marcus rightly pays for. He's looking a little rattled, his hair rumpled like he's run his hands through it. My heart pangs for him. It's gotta be rough to meet your kid just as you start to prep for your death. They exchange numbers and everything, and I wonder what's going to happen to Bash when he tries to call Marcus and the number is out of service.

Not my problem, I remind myself. I have my own stuff to worry about. Plus all my clients. I spend all day hearing people weep about the lives they're losing. I'm not wasting emotions on someone actively trying to rid themselves of mortality.

Still, he blinks hard in the late morning sun when we step into the street, his steps faltering.

"You okay?"

"Yes." He nods quickly – too quickly – and raises his arm to hail a cab. "I'm fine."

"Alright then. Guess I'll talk to you later."

His shocked eyes meet mine as a cab slides to a halt in front of him. It's the first sign of genuine emotion from him apart from what I saw with Bash, and my tummy flutters that I've elicited it from him. "What do you mean?"

"It's eleven in the morning. I've got work at nine. I've gotta get home, get some sleep."

"You're coming to my place."

"What for?"

His eyes slide left, then right. Oh, this vampire is fucked up, alright. "For safety. I need you where I can keep an eye on you until the curse is lifted. I can't risk anything happening to you."

"Nothing's going to happen to me."

"No. Because you'll be with me."

I roll my eyes. "I can't give up my life because you're scared I'll get mugged, Marcus. I need my clothes, my tooth-brush, my bed."

"You can have mine," he blurts.

"Your toothbrush?"

"Well, no, I'll get you a new one of those. New clothes too, if you like."

The cabbie toots the horn, impatient with us, and Marcus opens the door. "Get in, Kane."

He doesn't need to compel me. The idea of someone looking after me, even in the smallest way, is irresistible. I slide inside the cab and he follows me in, giving an address to the driver that has his attitude improving and my eyebrows rising.

"Nice part of town."

"It's rented."

The month's advance would equal my annual earnings but I keep my mouth shut, and twenty minutes later we're pulling into the driveway of a fuck-ugly mansion in a prestigious area of town.

"Did you not see pictures before you signed the rental agreement?"

Marcus sighs, his eyes closing briefly. "It was available and it was a steal. Apparently the former owner disappeared and the estate is renting it until they sell."

"Maybe the previous owner disappeared to avoid the shame of living in a house that looks like the gods abandoned a game of Tic-Tac-Toe with shipping containers."

"Your opinion has been noted," my vampire drawls. "However, maybe you could pry yourself away from judging the exterior and move inside? I'll be out of the sun, and I can assure you, you'll find many items inside to make snide comments about. I rented it furnished."

I follow him to the front door. "I thought the sun didn't bother you?"

"I won't burn to ash," Marcus admits. "But it's not pleasant. Gives me a roaring headache, and the longer I stay out the worse it gets."

"You're not going to choke to death on lasagne either?"

"If it were that easy, pet, I'd have no need for you."

The nickname does funny things to my stomach. I'm not sue if they're good feelings or not, but after months of feeling nothing, stuck in the endless numbing cycle of pain and paperwork that is health insurance, feeling something – anything – is like a flower blooming inside me. Bright, beautiful, and devastatingly fragile in the emotional wasteland it inhabits.

Sudden desperation seizes me to keep it alive. If Marcus can do that, can make me feel?

Hell, that's worth more than money.

Speaking of... "How much exactly do you think murdering you is worth? You haven't given me a number." I trail into the enormous house behind him, clutching my bag of scones.

Marcus treks all the way to the vast kitchen and sets down the books from Contreras Curiosities, pulling a bottle of sparkling water from the industrial sized refrigerator and holding it up with a questioning look.

"Got any still?" Water is taonga – treasure – on the island. The source of all life. The fuckery some people perform with it, carbon and flavour and additive shit, drives me up the wall. It's perfect the way it is, and we're lucky enough to have a decently clean supply of it here. Fizzy water. For fuck's sake.

He nods, and pulls out a jug, along with a blood bag.

"Where'd you get that?" I nod at the packet. "The last dude you approached in an alley?" I'm playing it off as a big joke, but the flower in my stomach droops a little at the idea of Marcus stalking other people, taking his pleasure and sustenance from them.

Am I a little fucked up? Yeah. But so's everyone else. At least I'm self-aware about it.

"Blood bank," he answered absently, pouring both our beverages into crystal goblets.

"They just sell it?" I'm AB+ so I've spent enough time lying down with a needle in my arm for the good of mankind rather than personal pleasure to be thrilled about the idea that it's being sold for profit to the undead.

"In a manner," Marcus replies. "I do need to compel employees to hand it over, but for every bag I take, I pay generously and compel three more humans to donate."

"And what about when you run out?"

His eyes flash golden again and a shock of desire shoots through me, settling between my thighs.

"Would you like to hear about how I track humans down and drink them, Kane?" The question is silk, floating through the air towards me and wrapping itself around my dick, tugging gently. I stiffen behind my jeans and Marcus's smile turns smug. "I can smell it, you know? When you're aroused."

Well, fuck. That I did not know.

"Yeah?" I manage. "What's it smell like, then?"

He moves faster than I can see, blood still sloshing in his glass on the marble counter where he left it when he runs his nose up the length of my throat. "Normally, human arousal is musky. Earthy. Like dirt on the bottom of a leather boot. Not something you track into the house. You keep it hidden in bedrooms and behind doors. Human shame around these things as a species is as predictable as it is childish. But you?" His nose travels the length of my neck again, inhaling deeply, and I almost pass out from the sensory overload of just being wanted. "Yours is sweeter."

"I'm a sweet guy," I manage, and his chuckle against my Adam's apple is almost enough of a vibration to get me off.

"Maybe," he murmurs. "But I think it's because you know the truth about me. The lack of deception makes your desire sweeter. You know what I am. You know you shouldn't want me. But you do. And that, pet, is the sweetest twist of all."

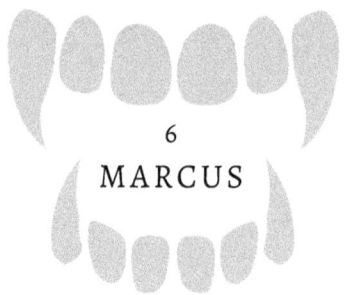

6

MARCUS

I hunted him like a wolf, and now he follows me like a lamb.

Perfect, perfect pet.

No, not pet. I shake my head sharply to dispel the thought. Prey.

Perfect prey.

I lead him by the hand to the bedroom. One of them. They all look the same, obnoxiously ostentatious. I enjoy the finer things in life, of course, as anyone with my heritage is wont to do. But money can't buy taste, and this place photographed a lot better than it looks in reality.

No matter. I am here for weeks, if that. The final night of the full moon is two nights away and I am hopeful Kane will be ready for the ceremony by then. If not, another month means little in the scheme of things.

In *my* scheme.

But I have been a patient man for a very long time. It is not unexpected that my desire for action rears its head as the finish line becomes clearer.

In fact, action is exactly what I need.

His words echo in my mind. "I'm a sweet guy."

I tug him around until he's facing me. "If you enter this room with me," I tell him, serious now, "there's no pulling out of the job. I can get sex from very many places, pet. But you are the only person in the world who can break the curse that binds me. If you have any doubt about your ability to separate professionalism and pleasure–"

"None," he assures me quickly, before I've even finished my sentence.

"None?"

A glib smile pulls at the corner of his full mouth. "Do you want references, mate? Should I tell you about all the coworkers I've fucked over the years?"

Anger flares inside me, and something more sinister, a darker rage than I'm used to. "That won't be necessary," I reply, and his grin widens enough that I know he's caught the snap in my tone.

I let the darkness coil around me though, let it drag me under even as I drag him through the door. Things might never be the same after the next few days, and I'll be damned if I let my last fuck be a bad one.

Especially when I've waited so long for it.

Hunting a single witch bloodline across the globe doesn't leave much time for recreational dick-wetting.

Now that my affairs are nearly in order, the business of an actual affair doesn't seem so insurmountable. And I've streamlined the process greatly with my body's unexpectedly determined attraction to Kane.

Fortunately, he appears to feel the same way, if the bulge in his jeans is any indicator.

Another indicator might be the way he shoves me up against the bedroom wall as soon as we're over the threshold.

"No vampire biting," he tells me seriously, gray eyes on mine. "That's a dealbreaker. Not just for sex, for all of it." I nod, desperation strumming a rapid reverb through me and he rewards me with one of those cocky, lazy smiles from earlier in the night.

"Good boy," he says, dropping a kiss on my nose like I'm a fucking Pomeranian and then he dance away, laughter snaking through the air behind him until I crash tackle him at super-speed, using one hand to cushion his head as we hit the mattress with unnatural force. Removing our clothes is part-wrestling, part calisthenics, all limbs and stretched cotton and foul language, and then it's over, the dim light sneaking around the shades just enough to make out the lines of his body.

Kane's not a small man. He's my height, similar breadth, with longer legs and a narrower waist. Lanky, loosely muscled, his hair mussed and flowing down to his shoulders. His cock matches, long and thick, gleaming at the swollen tip as he grips it and squeezes. "You want it?"

"Yeah, I fucking want it," I snarl. "I want all of you."

A tiny shudder runs through him, and heat licks at me in masculine pride. "Keep stroking it," I tell him. "Show me how you like it."

He does, grip tight, wrist loose, twisting his thumb over the darkened tip every time, collecting the liquid beads that gather there like pearls and using them to slick the glide of his hand up and down.

I wrap my hand around my own cock, squeezing like he did, then matching his timing. Stroke for stroke, the slapping sound in stereo as we wank in harmony, eyes glued to each other's pumping fists.

"Lube?" he gasps at one point, and I have to leave the bed to find it in my half-unpacked suitcase. I slip the lip open with my thumb, squeezing it into my waiting palm and switching hands as I kneel on the mattress next to him. The cool glide is bliss and I toss the tube his way.

"Get ready."

"You don't want me to…"

"We'll get to that. We'll get to everything."

This time, his grin is boyish relief, and my chest clenches. "You're gorgeous," he murmurs suddenly, the lube still clenched tightly in his fist. "Before this ends, before it even gets started, I want you to know that."

I startle briefly. I've been alive – in a fashion – for so long now, with so few acquaintances, that I can't remember the last time someone paid me a compliment that wasn't for a piece of clothing or a tip.

"You are too," I reply eventually, awkwardly, and he smiles again, not so wide this time.

The ache to see his true smile digs its claws into me. "Get ready, Kane," I urge, my voice lower. "I won't warn you again." I will, I'll warn him as many times as he needs. Hell, I'll apply the lube myself with my tongue if he wants, but the man who met me knife-first in an alley isn't going to put up with me trying to run the show and the best way to get him out of his head is to get his head focused on this thing between us.

Sure enough… "Why would you warn me?" he groans, even as he flips the cap open on his hip bone and squeezes the liquid into his hand.

I just stare at him and raise a brow. He's not a virgin, I'm sure of it, and I'm big. He winks at me softly. "Gotcha."

I leap on him, my cock brushing his leg as he squirms, choking on his own laughter. "Got you," I murmur quietly, and dip my head to take his mouth.

He's cool to the taste, mint mixing with the marzipan, and when he runs his tongue along the seam of my lips I relax, letting him slip inside. We stay like that for long, drugging moments. Naked and making out. His hands explore my back, my shoulders, trip-tickle along my ribs. I nip (fangless) at the spot beneath his ear, then capture his bottom lip between my teeth, tugging on it as I stare down into his silver-shot eyes until he reaches down and slides his fist in an agonising single pass up and down my throbbing cock.

"Put it in," he whispers against my mouth.

"You didn't get ready," I whisper back, and the grin is back. I cheer internally.

"That's your job, mate. You want to fuck my ass? You gotta prep it."

I'm nothing if not diligent, so I set to work, pleasure spiking my skull at the sound Kane makes when I slip one finger inside his hole, then the second. The moan he lets out when I scissor them gently, stretching him to take me, has me climbing his body again, pressing kisses across the top of his chest as my fingers keep at their essential task.

And it is essential. This close to Kane, that I can smell the salt of him on his skin, catch his hitched breaths in my mouth? Having him is suddenly the most critical event imaginable.

"Condom?" he gasps as I withdraw my finger slowly, taking a moment to lick up the crease of his balls.

"Vampires can't host human diseases," I tell him. "I've got nothing, and nothing you might have could get to me either. Let me ride you bareback, pet. I promise I'll make it good."

He shudders out a tense laugh. "That was never in doubt."

Pride has me leaking in my own hand as I reapply lube. We lock eyes for a second as I position myself between his spread knees.

"Don't judge," I warn him.

Then I spit in my hand and rub it right onto his puckered entrance.

"Marcus!" The top half of his body jackknifes up from the mattress as he folds himself, trying to see his own asshole.

"Vampire saliva has anesthetic properties," I assure him. "It numbs the area slightly and can increase pleasure."

"Still," he grumbles, "warn a guy before you–"

I press my thumb inside, deep, and his eyes go hazy. "Ohhh."

"Yes," I smile. "Oh. Hold your knees apart for me."

He does, bless him, the thick meat of his cheeks separating and giving me full access to that coveted hole. I settle the tip of my dick against it, pressing forward, watching the soft give of his flesh swallow mine whole.

"Gods!" Kane's voice cracks brokenly through the air above us as my hipbones meet his skin. "That feels *incredible.*"

He feels incredible, warm and tight and perfect, just like I knew he would be. But I can't say that, so I just ease out, then rock forward again, a gentle cadence designed to titillate, not to tip either one of us over the edge.

It doesn't work like that, though. Kane reaches out blindly, grabbing at my forearm, and a sharp pain ricochets up my arm. I snap my head down and catch sight of the droplets, studded along my skin like tiny rubies.

Blood.

Something shifts in me, my whole psyche standing up and moving four feet to the left inside my skull, and now there's something else there in the empty part. It's me, but not the me I see in the mirror. Me from another perspective, through someone else's eyes.

Through *Kane's* eyes.

I can see myself staring down, hair pushed back as I work myself in and out of him. My hair, my face, my body, sweat beading as I stare down at myself through Kane.

The whole thing jolts and then it's gone and I'm looking down at him the same way we were.

"Did you see that?"

"Yeah."

"You know what it was?"

"No. You?"

"No idea. Want to keep going?"

"Fuck, yes." He lifts his hips as he says it, sending me deeper, and a hot bolt of ecstasy drive deep into the base of my spine.

The not-mirror image appears again, fainter this time, hovering on the outside.

"It's back," I pant between thrusts, moving harder now.

"I don't care," he says, blonde hair spread out across the pillow as he arches upwards. "You're hot, I'm hot, it's hot. It'll be a blood bond thing. Just ignore it."

Except I can't, because he's right, it is hot, watching us like this, like we're a film cut into different moments, feeling it and seeing it all at once. And when Kane reaches down and grasps his own cock, pulling on it with fast, hard strokes and I feel that as well?

I explode.

Kane follows me over the edge a moment later, his release soaking us both as I let the constant weight go and fall down into his soft heat, dick still buried inside the sweet ass that will haunt my dreams until my dying day.

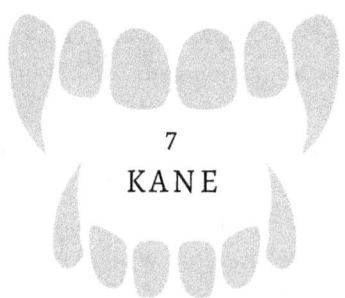

7

KANE

*E*veryone wonders how they'll die.

Some people, upon meeting a vampire, might assume it'd be by having your blood drunk.

I'm empty of a range of bodily fluids, but my blood isn't one of them. Yet, anyway.

Gods Almighty, Marcus can fuck. The true threat to humans expiring in vampire company isn't the blood-sucking, its dehydration.

"Dying," I mumble into the pillows after our third round. "Need water." He pries himself away from me, sweat and other liquids creating a sticky web seeking to bond our bodies together, and his footsteps disappear down the hall. He's back a few minutes later – impressive, really, considering the size of the place – and the quiet thunk of a glass on the beside table next to me has me opening fuck-drunk eyes and pushing my bedhair out of them so I can see the precious life force for myself.

It's still. Thank the gods. Though I'm desperate enough to drink sparkling, a sure sign of how far I've fallen.

As if coming all over the cock of my ancestors' enemy isn't enough.

Owner of said cock and my ancestors' wrath settles onto the mattress beside me, one hand trailing over my spine in languid passes. It feels too good, too intimate, despite the things we've already done, but I can't find it in myself to shake him off. Just lie there and gulp my water, pretending this is a normal one-nighter (nooner?) and I'm not going to murder the undead sex god who I've apparently mindmelded with via orgasm.

Just the usual.

"What are you thinking about?" Marcus does not appear to be a fan of avoidance.

I place my glass carefully on the coaster. "Killing you."

"Hmmm. Have you worked out how to do it?"

"Almost." I flipped through some of the more hopeful looking books in the taxi here. They kickstarted my memory, droplets of long-lost knowledge trickling back into my consciousness, winding a shining blue magic arc through the tunnels of my mind where I'd tucked other stored parts of history and healer lore. I'm not there yet. Fi was right – confidence is all well and good, but fucking around with this stuff is a fool's game if you don't know what you're doing. For all I know, I could end up stuck with Marcus for eternity due to a rogue crystal or mispronunciation.

Fuck around and immortal out.

Least I wouldn't have to worry about being boned to death. Mind you, my relationships are not known for their longevity. If I left Makutu to avoid seeing Iakopo Powers in temple on Sundays after his sister caught him giving me a handy under the wharf, I'm sure as shit not down to be crossing spiritual paths with an ex-fling on the eternal regular.

"I'd prefer to do it sooner rather than later," he says, and despite my very logical mind-thoughts, my stomach hollows.

"Sure." I force lightness into my voice. "Expedient expiration. Got it. Do you want me to get started now, or…"

"Later will be fine." I'm not a fan of the dry amusement threading Marcus's tone. "Why don't you tell me more about your family?"

"Why?"

"Mākutu has always fascinated me. More so since the curse. How a place, a people, so powerful could go undetected for so long. Even now, few know of it, and even fewer know of its secrets."

Can't hurt. There's nobody from Tauhoe left but me, and he'll be dead soon enough.

"Simple enough story. No dad, Mum died when I was a kid. She and Kuia were already raising me, so Kuia finished the job."

"You didn't want to stay with her?"

I shrug, rolling over to face him. "I wanted to help people but not in the same way." I hesitate, then figure, what the hell? If anyone knows what it's like to be an outsider it's probably the 150-year-old vampire aristocrat slumming it in Apex City with his witchy toyboy murderer. "I've never felt quite like I belong on the island. I don't look the same as everyone else, for one." He tilts his head in acknowledgement. The Polynesian aesthetic is strong in Mākutu, which was settled by the Moriori and then Māori invaders who intermixed with the indigenous folk. My dirty blond hair and gray eyes are about as far as you can get from fitting in physically, thanks to my no-good father and his dominant gene pool. "So all the time I was training to be a healer with Kuia, there were some people who didn't want me to practice on them. Not even the smallest things, salves for insect bites, herbs to stop a fever. I was just a kid when I started training, five or six. It knocked my confidence, you know. And then my mum died." I shrug again, because what else can you do? Those are my emotional support shrugs. They've been my constant companion these twenty years or more. "On an island of six hundred people, death is a big deal. And Kuia and I couldn't save her. A lot of people had already written Mama off cos she went to the mainland and came back pregnant with me, no man in sight."

"You never heard from your father?" There's no judgement in the question, just light curiosity, but my shoulders crawl towards my ears anyway.

"No." *A jumped-up slayer with too many ideals and not enough integrity*, Kuia told me one night after Mama's funeral when she'd had a few too many. He'd stayed in Sydney looking down the stake of a short lifespan but happy to die a hero rather than play father to a bastard born in the back isles of nowhere. How would he feel now, I wonder, to know his offspring is about to slay a centurion and a half without a whisper of training from him and his ilk? Oh, Kuia made sure I knew how to fight, knew the techniques, but Marcus will be my first kill. On Mākutu, healing comes before hurt, every time.

It's why Marcus is still alive, despite the inconvenience he's claimed it causes him. Mākutu lore calls to restore the relationships that have been strained. Between our people and the ocean, the ocean and the land, the tribes that weave from village to village, and individuals themselves. My ancestors cursed Marcus hoping he would see the error of his ways and make amends, not merely to punish him.

It's who we are. It's why we've survived.

Individualism is a flawed notion, and flawed notions in power lead to unimaginable devastation. Kings, conquerors, autocrats, and assholes. Every one of them fed by the hand of individualism until they grow too big no one individual can control them.

I have my own demons, but that isn't one of them. My father, for all that he can be called that, didn't understand the ways of Mākutu. And that's his loss. As am I.

"What was your father like?" I ask instead, and Marcus pauses, long fingers tangled in my hair.

"He was fair," he says finally. "To us, at least. His children, his wife. Not particularly warm, as men in that time weren't. He never knew of my proclivities, of course–" he gestures towards me. I am unreasonably delighted to be identified as a proclivity. Old-ass English words have a way of making even implied insults sound impressive. " – and I took great pains to keep it that way. But he played games with us fairly often, taught me about business and finance, and every Sunday after church he would buy sweetmeats for my mother, sister and I from an elderly woman who had lost her husband years before and turned to baking to make a living."

"You had a sister?"

He smiles, a brief flash of unimaginable beauty. "Caroline. She was beautiful. Kind, intelligent, an excellent pianist. Two years older than me, and I adored her. Father arranged for her to be married to a horrid man not long after I turned."

"You kept up with them once you were busy murdering everyone in the ton?"

"I did. I murdered her husband."

My eyes, which have slipped shut as he plays with my hair, fly open. "You *what*?"

"I murdered him. Before he could breed her. Caroline would have been an excellent mother, but that man's child would have kept her indentured to the family well past his death. Being a childless widow gave her more freedom, and she escaped to the country claiming mourning. After an appropriate amount of time, I selected a kind man from a good family, a second son, and proceeded to encourage their courtship."

"You–" I lift my head off the cushion of his shoulder, incredulous. "You used your vampire powers to act as a *matchmaker for your sister?*"

"Quite. Their marriage seemed to be a happy one. They had four children, lived comfortably and died within months of each other just prior to the war."

"Which war?"

"*Which*... the Great War!"

"The first one?"

"Yes, the first one!"

"You can't blame me for being confused, Marcus. You've lived through a ton of wars." I grin at him to let him know I'm teasing, and he relaxes somewhat. "Anyway," he continues, only slightly huffy. "My mother passed of influenza not long after, she lived to a mighty age. My father died in a spirited cricket match with my nephews while visiting my sister around the turn of the twentieth century, I believe."

"That sounds like a good way to go, I suppose," I offer hesitantly. "Probably a bit traumatic for the kids, though."

"They were both in their twenties by then. We Grosvenors have never known when to quit."

"Except you."

"Except me," he agrees, looking down at me with those brown eyes. "I do what must be done."

"Hot," I whisper, waggling my brows at him and he huffs out a laugh.

"If you say so."

"I do. In fact," I slide down the sheet and cup his hardening flesh in my hand, "I think your dedication to follow through should be rewarded."

"That doesn't make sense. I'm asking you to–"

"It doesn't need to make sense, Marcus," I interrupt. "I'm

trying to segue into sucking your cock. Let me have this, hmm?"

"If you insist," he replies, the last word cracking on a moan as I lap the underside of his cock, tracing the thick vein with my tongue. "Fuck, Kane, the way you look…"

I know exactly how I look, I can see it in my mind's eye, the blood bond surging through us, weaving our experience together in one frenetic, fractured, pleasure-drenched haze. I see myself circle his tip, the pink of my tongue almost perfectly matching the delicate mushroom of his flesh. I feel the twist of his fingers in my hair, guiding me, even as the image flashes behind my closed lids. Then I press a soft kiss to his slit and the kick of pleasure laced with anticipation echoes in my own balls as Marcus's hips jerk and he urges me in low tones to do it again. I do, several times, and then I reach up and he sucks my fingers into his mouth. Through the bond I can feel the care he's taking not to scratch me with his incisors, can feel even those, stretching and lengthening in the corresponding pressure along my own upper jaw. I smear Marcus's saliva around my mouth, making a mess, sure to lubricate the corners where my lips meet so they won't crack under the strain. Then I take him fully in my mouth, sinking down, holding my breath until my nose bumps the soft bristle of his pubic hair and then I exhale, catching my breath once more and tightening my lips, my throat, around the thickness of his dick.

"Oh fuck yes," he hisses, and Marcus swearing while he's buried inside me is so godsdamned sexy I almost lose it right there. The high of making this man break his precious propriety rules is a rush like no other. "You sexy fucking man. Swallowing my cock like you were born for it."

I was born for this, I think dreamily, the endorphins lighting me up like Guy Fawkes inside. I flex my tongue, sucking now, long, deep pulls, not bobbing my head, just letting my tongue and throat work him like the tides, rolling in and out from the same spot, the hand that isn't clutching his roughly haired thigh sneaking underneath so I can press my thumb against his perineum.

Marcus's laugh is dark and a little unhinged and he rocks his hips, settling that perfectly smooth spot more firmly against my digit. I redouble my efforts with my mouth and his praise rattles from him in rib-shaking exhalations.

"Who's a good pet? Just like that. You know what you're doing, don't you? Ahhh, that sweet fucking mouth. Taking me so good."

I bathe in his praise, wrapping it around me like a shimmering blanket as I work him, mouth and hand in tandem. He swells even more in my mouth and I should tap, should take a break, but I can't, I *can't*. Nothing on Earth matters to me more in this instant than breaking Marcus down until he's nothing but flesh made lightning and bone made gold. I stroke him gently with my thumb, let it slide up and brush over the tight pucker tempting me and he shouts. Both his hands are in my hair now, wrapping it around his fists and he's moving me, slamming my willing mouth up and down his stiff flesh and I have seconds, milliseconds, where I can breathe, so I do, I suck deeply in through my nose and chase his cock with my tongue. I let it drag against the underside as he fucks my mouth, licking where I can, letting it ride the punishing rhythm of Marcus's thrusts to heighten the sensation and I can *feel* it. Feel the way he feels, watching me, feeling me, hot and wet and willing and eager. And through him, I can feel him feeling it too, tasting himself on my tongue, the burn of my lips, the sting of tears in my eyes and the giddy euphoria dancing through my veins. My own dick is hard enough to pound diamonds just from this vicarious connection and I straddle one big leg and grind myself on Marcus's thigh, precum spilling down and easing my slide into a delicious, dirty rasp that reaches directly into the back of my brain and unlocks something until I'm humping his leg like its the key to fucking life.

"Jesus, fuck," Marcus chokes out, and I open my eyes, my gaze smashing into his as I tighten my mouth and slide my thumb up, bypassing the ring of muscle and burying deep inside him.

"You. Perfect. Little. Fuck." Marcus snarls, everything inside him tightening and I inhale through my nose, curl my thumb, and throw my head down, cramming him deep inside my throat and humming.

Marcus curses a blue streak, hips bucking like a rodeo steer, and I ride him out. His fingers tighten in my hair, lighting up every nerve ending I have and then he's coming, thick and salty-sweet down my throat and I'm right there with him, experiencing it through his mind and my own and I'm coming too, eyes squeezed shut as I crash through time and space and memories in a holographic kaleidoscope, pleasure fracturing my mind and body into sharp shards of blood-edged pleasure, Marcus right there with me in the vortex.

8

MARCUS

*W*hen I was a young boy, my father would take me with him on hunting trips. Other men scoffed at his softness, although I certainly never saw it as such. Hunting is not for the weak. Even if you catch nothing, you leave parts of yourself along the way. You shed what you no longer need, or if not that it is stripped from you.

Blood and fabric, plenty of both left on thorns or ragged gate posts. Your time, your playfulness. Your innocence certainly. To the ways of the wild and the ways of the bedroom, as told by men in groups.

Hunting, by its very nature, makes you strong.

So strong that it can be easy to forget that in the wildness of the world, the hunter can also become the prey.

Kane has dragged me – reluctantly, I admit – out of bed and into the city again. He has an idea he wants to run past Filomena, something he claims could unlock the curse. Apparently it came to him while he slept, and he sat bolt upright in bed, hair everywhere, eyes silver in the early morning moonlight and exclaimed, "Fuck me dead, I've got it."

While I've more than proven I'm willing to fuck him as a dead man, he wasn't distracted by my advances, instead rolling out of bed with the vigour of an elite athlete and tossing me my pants. "Get dressed. We've got to talk to Fi."

"It's four in the morning," I pointed out. After much, much debating, a sizeable deposit and a thorough rimming, Kane had finally agreed to call in sick to work last night, which pleased me to no end. Unfortunately as a nocturnal creature, I'd spent most of the night staring at him while he slept, only grateful that his work ethic and enthusiasm for sexual activities had left him too exhausted to wake and spot me staring at him like a lovestruck heroine in a moving picture.

If he knew what he meant to me… what his lifting the curse will do? He would never speak to me again. The saints will forgive me for taking a little time to appreciate the good in this world before I burn it all down.

"Heat up some of my scones, would ya?" he called from the bathroom over the sound of running water, the flat vowels of his accent melding together in an almost-indistinguishable word. *Hedupsoomamascoanswoodyah?*

It should be irritating, but it's not. It's charming, and I'm irritated about that instead.

He's still chattering away now, in the car ride towards the city, asking the driver about his family. Oh, look. Here come the kids pictures, tucked into the man's wallet. The scent of warm leather fills the car, mixing with my shampoo (on Kane), my shirt (ditto) and the sour tang of my own jealousy on my tongue.

I want him to be talking to me.

It's irrational, and inconvenient, and this will end in a bloodbath of some description, but for the time we have on Earth together, this man and I, I want to be the only one he's talking to, looking at, smiling for.

Hunting Kane, it seems, has not made me strong. It has made me unhinged.

And it's only a matter of time until he realises.

Strength is a fine quality when it stands alone. Coupled with madness, it's a recipe for disaster.

You know what to do, the annoying conscience Kane's ancestors drove into my psyche reminds me. You could tell him the truth.

Fuck off, I think back, and they launch into peals of laughter, a regular Greek chorus.

I sulk all the way to midtown, then refrain from launching myself over the seat and ripping our cab driver's throat out when we pull to a stop. Instead, I tip him twenty percent instead of my usual thirty, and ignore his cheery farewell. Kane, obviously, is already fast friends with him and wishes him peace in Arabic before slamming the door shut.

"You know Arabic?"

"I know the basics. Here." He pulls me to a stop at a souvenir kiosk and hands me a pair of cheap sunglasses off the rotating stand by the 'I Heart Apex City' t-shirts.

"I have sunglasses." *Nice* sunglasses.

"Cool. Where?"

I open my mouth, then pause. I've left them at home, along with my well-crafted plan and my common sense. "Not here."

"Then take these," he waggles them at me. "I don't want you getting a sun-migraine and being an even bigger dick than you were to the cabbie."

"I wasn't a dick to the cabbie."

"You were dickish for *you*." He tucks the glasses into the pocket of my button-down and turns to pay for them before I can comprehend how in a single day he's managed to learn me quite so well as to identify my so-called dickishness.

The sun's still barely peeking around the arched glass and steel of the highrises, but I slide them on my face regardless. Being given a gift, no matter how small, is a novelty.

"Cute," Kane appears at my elbow, matching sunglasses on his own face. "Now we're twins."

I ignore that. "Would you like a coffee?" I didn't have any at the house, I didn't care for it before the change and even less after. Kane had a tea, but I could tell he was mostly drinking it to be polite.

"Gods yes." He leads me to a coffee shop near the building I met him at last night and orders the same sugar-based milky concoction masquerading as coffee as yesterday to go. We wander towards Contreras Curiosities, looking into windows and sidestepping signs as the retail sector of the city starts to come alive.

"She's unlikely to be there," I point out, not for the first time.

"Maybe," Kane replies, and I wonder if he's tapping into some kind of magical intuition, or just winging this whole thing. He certainly seemed determined when he woke up this morning. "Either way, you can hang out with your kid again." He shoots me a sly look from behind his to go cup.

"I'm not thrilled about that choice of wording."

"Is that a vamp thing? Not keen on having a grown man call you Daddy?"

"Depends on the man," I growl, and he throws his head back and laughs, the early morning light picking out the gold in his hair.

"My own sire was negligent," I admit when he's wiped tears of amusement from the corners of his eyes. "And then I repeated the pattern. I have many complicated feelings about Sebastian. He sees me as saving his life, and I did to an extent I suppose given that he was in the middle of dying of a drug overdose at the time. But this new life, this half-life between the dead and the living?" I raise my arms and gesture around us. "Some wouldn't call it a life at all."

"So why do it?"

I hesitate in answering. I know why of course, I've had years to marinate on this very point. But telling Kane feels like it crosses a line of some kind. One deeper than sex or murder. "Because I couldn't just watch another human die senselessly."

Kane doesn't say anything, just gives a low 'hmmm,' and I suddenly want him to understand. "I watched humans do so for years, caused many senseless deaths myself. But after the curse, nothing. The regret was too raw, the consequences too painful. To live this life is one thing, but to live it in active suffering? That's a unique kind of torture. Yet after I turned Sebastian, that's all I could feel. Suffering. Guilt. The curse come to life inside my blood. Even when my logic prevailed and told me I'd saved him, the curse reminded me I'd caused him more harm than good. That's when I began seeking a cure."

Kane doesn't say anything, just nods and digs his little silver smoke machine out of the pocket of his jeans. The marzipan cloud surrounds me, heralding the sound of the pianoforte and the sweetness of sugar on my tongue again, before it's gone and it's just Kane and I in an Apex City alley in the fading dawn.

It happens in slow motion. Four men, young but not young enough not to know better. Two from each end, moving quickly. Kane's reflexes are impressive for a human – his knife flashes through the air, piercing the forearm of one and giving the second a moment's pause. My human takes advantage of his opponent's weakness, stepping over the man's fallen brethren and pressing the steel blade against the second man's neck.

The other two are almost on me, and it's almost embarrassing for them how easy it is. I move quickly, not bothering to temper my speed for their fragile human brains to process. Dislocated knees, both of them, and they fall to the filthy alley floor, cries rising in the morning air. I pick one up by the neck, and slam him face-first into the alley wall. Blood springs to life in the air around me, calling my name in an irresistible lure as it gushes from its hosts crooked nose. The other man rolls towards where I hold his comrade, grabbing for my ankle and I kick him in the face, hard. His head snaps back, body slackening, and then he doesn't move again. Kane and the bigger man are still on the opposite wall, Kane's knife clutched in their combined grip as they struggle for dominance.

Shit.

I lick would-be attacker's face, the sweet tang of blood fresh from the source sizzling through my system, then drop him into a crumpled heap next to his friend. In seconds I have the knife in my hand and Kane at my back as I deliver five sharp punctures to the man. He screams, the shock preventing him from attempting to escape more than any damage I may have caused. He's huge, and I'm momentarily impressed my little witch fared so easily against him, especially when I smell the synthetic anabolics tainting his blood.

Steroids. They make you big, but they make you slow. And stupid.

"Who are you?" I ask, pushing my voice into his head so he can hear me over his own pitiful squawking.

"Nobody," he garbles out past a mouthful of snot and saliva.

"Don't be silly," I say silkily. "Everybody has a name. What's yours?"

"I'm nobody," he chokes out again, and I sigh. Pulling back I grasp his chin and jerk his head up. No point in him watching his own blood paint the alley floor, it'll only distract him from my questions. I wait until he's looking right at me, then trigger the compulsion. "What's your name?"

"Rodney Walter."

"Lovely. And why have you chosen to attack us on such a pretty morning, Rodney?"

"Money," he sobs.

"Is someone paying you to do this?" He shakes his head frantically.

"I see. An enterprising group of peers, then. Do you do this often?"

"Yeah," comes the grunted reply.

"And what happens to the money?"

"We split it."

"Do you have a wife? Children?" Another head shake. "Do they?" I tilt my head towards the various members of his crew, all in various stages of consciousness with their limbs askew or bleeding.

"No. None of us. I got a whore I see sometimes."

"A sex worker."

"Yeah, a whore."

I sigh. "Sex worker is the appropriate title, Rodney. Use it."

"Yes, sir."

"And you pay them fairly?"

"I guess. She picks the price. Sometimes I tip."

"Sometimes?!"

I shoot a look back at Kane. He's watching us carefully, no sign whether he'll help me toss these bodies in the Dumpster or run for his life. "Can I kill him?"

"Dunno." His voice is casual but his next question isn't. "Can you live with yourself if you do?"

Ugh.

I turn back to Rodney and flash my fangs. The distinct smell of fresh urine fills the air.

"You're lucky you didn't try this shit tomorrow," I hiss at him. "Here's what you're going to do. You're going to take all the money you've made robbing people and give a third of it to your sex worker. Then you're going to delete her number and leave her in peace. The rest of the money will be…" I rack my brain, trying to come up with something I can say in front of Kane, because the truth is, I'd usually take it myself.

"You're going to donate to a lady named Joyce Talbolt." Kane's voice comes from behind me. "She lives in West Acre Retirement Community. You're going to tell her that it's to help cover her husband's medical care. And then you're going to apply for a job at Eternal Life Assurance in the call centre. Make some money the old-fashioned way."

I repeat the words, weighting them with compulsion, and Rodney nods along like one of those silly little dashboard dog.

"What about his friends?" Kane asks.

"And you're going to convince your friends to donate their money to charity and apply to the call centre as well. Tell them that you came close to losing your life on this job when a piece of scaffolding fell down on you in this alley." I hold my free hand up so he can see the barest sliver of light between my thumb and forefinger, "And you're not prepared to risk it any longer."

"Yes, sir."

"Anything else?" I ask Kane over my shoulder.

"No." He pauses. "Did you want a drink?"

"Not this one. This one's on the roids. Maybe that one." I point to the man Kane initially slashed with his knife, and his eyes widen. He tries to scramble backward, clutching his bleeding arm to his chest.

"Go on, then," Kane says. "Just make sure he doesn't remember it."

I drop Rodney, who starts frantically mumbling 'Joyce Talbolt, West Acre Retirement Community' to himself and pulls out his phone to type something in, and turn to Kane, who's watching me with steady eyes. "Are you sure?"

"This is who you are, Marcus." He says it with utmost calm. "This is who you've been for over a century. You're the one trying to change yourself, not me. But no killing, yeah? That's the line for me."

I nod once, my chest expanding. "Noted."

Thug #1 makes a renewed effort to escape, but it's no use. I don't bother with the trance to ease his pain. He certainly didn't bother to be polite when he attacked my witch. I sink my fangs into his carotid artery and suck him down in greedy glugs. His blood is sweet with a hint of spice – cinnamon, maybe. He tastes like apple tarts and the absolute *freedom* of being able to enjoy human blood from the source in front of someone has me reluctant to stop.

But I promised Kane, so I do, pulling back slowly, swallowing the last remnants in my mouth and running my tongue over the holes I've left to seal them and begin the healing process.

"What's your name?" I ask my meal, as I maneuver him to a propped up position against the alley wall.

"Paul," he replies dazedly. The shock's hitting him now, the euphoria, too, that can come with the bite. Not all humans experience it, but enough.

"How old are you?"

"Twenty-four."

"You're a good boy, Paul," I tell him, patting his paled cheek. "Stay out of trouble."

"Okay," he slurs, eyes closing.

"Was that a compulsion?" Kane asks from beside me.

"Just a little one. There's a psychic link that exists while feeding. It allows us to read our food's energy levels, know when we've taken enough. It fades over time, but sometimes just a reminder is enough to keep someone on the right path."

"You're a strange man, Marcus Goodfella."

My lips curl as we make our way out of the alley. The sun is brighter now, and I slip the cheap sunglasses from the souvenir stand from where they hang in my collar and slide them on over my eyes. "You're not the first to say so, pet."

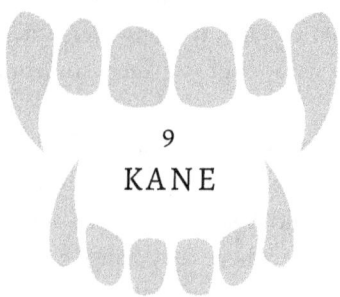

9

KANE

Fi is, as I suspected, in the shop when we arrive an hour prior to opening.

Like recognises like, and having a vampire roll in with his would-be witch murderer would be enough to get me into study-mode on curiosity alone, so it's no surprise that she flings the door open when we knock and ushers us inside.

"Lemon balm tea?" She holds up the pot like she's on Wheel of Fortune. "Good for clarity of mind."

We both take a cup, me because I spilt my coffee in our alley scuffle, and Marcus to be polite, I think. He's a peculiar man, even accounting for the vampirism and his age. I can't quite work him out, and it niggles at me. Working out problems, what's causing them, how to solve them, is the whole point of being a healer, no matter what culture I practice in. He has so many symptoms that don't seem to add up, but I haven't nutted out the root cause yet. There's something missing, the final piece that will slot into place and give me my Marcus Diagnosis.

If there's even time for that.

"I'm glad you're here," Fi says, once we're both situated

with our steaming mugs of lemon balm tea. Mine's in a giant pink mug designed to look like a cauldron with 'Witch's Brew' stamped on the side, and Marcus is attempting to look dignified while sipping his from one decorated with a cartoonish tarot card that depicts a satyr with an enormous erection looking at a newspaper. The card detail at the bottom reads 'You're Fucked.' I am disproportionally delighted by this.

"I was up all night going over the texts," Fi continues, and I feel a pang of guilt because I'm the one being paid for this and the only thing I was up all night doing was Marcus. "And there's a chance that if we use magnolia blossoms–"

"Yes!" I break in, sitting straight up. "The magnolia blossoms! As a substitute for the Mākutu ginger!" The thought had slammed into me while I slept, dragging me from slumber and insisting on bringing Marcus into the city immediately.

On the plus side, at least he'd had a hearty breakfast. He'd declined one of my scones before we left.

"The best option is obviously to take Marcus to the island," I continue, ignoring the slight cough from beside me that I assume is Marcus forcing down another mouthful of tea. For an English man, he does not appear to be keen on sampling all the different varietals his people went to so much trouble to secure rights to. The irony. "But the ginger season there hasn't started yet, and production has decreased significantly due to deforestation in the higher regions."

"Why can't we just use another kind of ginger?" Marcus asks, but I'm already shaking my head.

"Mākutu ginger is the best in the world. That's why it's so rare. The growing process gives it this unique golden color, almost like turmeric. We will be using ginger in the ceremony, but since it's not from Mākutu we need something else to boost its properties."

"It's not magnolia season here, either," Fi points out.

"Hothouse magnolias will do. Are there any in the glasses at Memorial Park?"

"I'll check." Fi pulls out her phone.

I turn to Marcus, who is watching me with an assessing gaze. "You're making good progress."

"Yeah." I grin at him. The muscle I felt unfurling when I walked in here yesterday is reaching out, seeking. The magic is coming back to me, slowly but steadily. And if the vine of magic strangles the strange blooming flower in my stomach I get when Marcus smiles at me? Well, at least I'll be left with one of them. "The best thing to do is to travel back to the island though."

"No." Marcus's tone is firm. "I don't want to wait that long. I want it done as soon as possible."

"I don't know how long you think flights take, but–"

"Tonight," he declares, standing and pouring his tea into an innocent potted aloe while Fi scrolls hothouse details on her phone. "With the two of you working together, that should be plenty of time."

"To– are you serious? A ceremony like this could take weeks to prepare."

"Tonight," he repeats. "I need to get back to the house and get my affairs in order. I'll be back at 7 p.m. Does that give you enough time, Fi?"

"Hmm?" Fi's head pops up. "That should be fine, lovely. I'll tell Bash and Mira so they can pop in and say goodbye. Plenty of magnolias in the hothouse at Memorial," she tells me. "I'll close the store for the day and we can prepare."

"I… I…" I slam my mouth shut. This is what I'm being paid for. This is what Marcus wants. It's why I'm here. Even if he's gorgeous as sin, compels scumbags into covering medical debt and fucks like a god, there's no need to get sentimental about it. I've had ex-lovers ghost me before, but not to the point of actually leaving the mortal coil. But this is Apex City, I guess. Everything seems brighter here. Even rejection.

"Sure," I say finally, because both Fi and Marcus are looking at me like I'm holding them up. "See you at seven. I'll be the one ready to murder you."

"Appreciate it, pet." And then he's gone.

"Whew," Fi watches the swinging door. "If I didn't have a strict humans-only policy... Right lovely, where were we? More tea?"

"Yeah, Fi," I drain my mug and try to swallow my sorrows down too. "More tea would be great."

———

My phone rings while Fi is out nicking magnolia blossoms from the city gardens.

"Kia ora?"

"Kanu," my cousin Arihi's voice is low and quick. "Has Marcus found you?"

"So you know about Marcus? How did I miss a whole vampire story from the elders? Is this one of the things you all talked about around the kava bowl while Kuia and I were working our fingers to the bone making poultices?"

"Kanu, this is serious." Arihi is not playing around. "Is he there? Has he found you?"

"Well, yeah."

"Fuck. Okay. Okay." She exhales heavily, breathing her anxiety right through the phone line and into me. It slides down my spine, tightening each vertebrae it meets until I'm cemented in place, my whole focus narrowed to my phone.

"What do you mean, 'fuck'?" I demand. "We knew vampires were real."

"We know vampires are real because of *Marcus*," Arihi

shoots back. "Because he came to Mākutu and tried to enslave our people."

"But our ancestors cursed him," I point out. "I'm not denying what he did was wrong, but he wasn't successful."

"It's a blood curse, Kanu," Arihi fires at me. "Think about what that means."

"It means only a member of the bloodline can lift it," I reply. "Marcus already explained that."

"Marcus already *explained* that? Jesus *Christ*, Kanu, how dense can you be? Have you forgotten everything Kuia taught you?"

"It's not a big deal, Ari. I just have to lift the curse. I know I'm out of practice, but there's a great shop here that has everything I need, and I've been reading up on the ceremony."

"The ceremony that you *die* in!" my cousin screeches down the phone. "You have to die to break a blood bond curse, Kanu! While the blood still flows through the line, the magic holds. It's only broken when there's nobody left."

Pain prickles at my temples, and I shake my head, trying to clear it. "That can't be true. You're still alive, Auntie, and Koro Silver–"

"We're too far removed," Ari interrupts. "We're not first cousins. You're the last of the Tauhoe line. Believe me, I've spent the last eighteen hours talking to every person on this island to find out what they know about Marcus, about the curse. If there were any secret babies that could alter this. I even called Dean."

Our asshole cousin Dean moved to Brisbane after Covid. Everyone hates Dean.

I scramble back through my brain, and she's right. Cousin-status has no place on the island. There's no first, no fourth, no fourteenth-twelve-times-removed-and-remarried-on-your-uncle's-side. Like most Polynesian cultures, you're either related or you're not. Arihi and I are cousins, but she's not directly from the Tauhoe line. *Nobody* else is.

The missing piece.

"He told me," I say faintly. "He told me I was the last one."

"You're the last one he needs to die," Arihi says solemnly. "Once that happens, the curse is lifted. He can come back here and take control of the whole island. Compel us all to do his bidding. There's nobody strong enough to stop him."

Fuck. Fuck, fuck, fucking fuckhole. What have I done?

"A plane." I blurt. "He paid me a deposit last night. I can catch a cab to the airport right now–"

"End the call, Kanu."

Marcus.

I squeeze my eyes tight, and he laughs, that smoky dark sound that turned me on last night turning me frozen with fear now in the wake of Arihi's call.

"Kanu? Kanu, are you still there? Kanu, answer me, you fucking knob jockey!" Despite her words I can hear the crack of tears in her voice, panic humming through the line. *She knows.* Without me saying a word, she knows.

"Oh, pet. I don't have to look into your eyes to compel you. Not when you've let me in so many other places." Each word is a drop of poison onto my skin, spreading shame and despair across my skin like uninhabitable bush, too thick to hack through to find anything else beneath.

He's here to kill me. And I slept with him.

"End the call, Kanu."

"Love you, Ari," I whisper into the phone. "Say bye to Auntie."

She's still screaming when I hang up.

"Start the ceremony."

"The magnolia–"

"You don't need the fucking flowers. Do it now."

I turn my head and look at him. He's as beautiful as the

first time I saw him. Dark hair, diamond jaw, golden-brown eyes.

"Why couldn't we go to the island?"

That pretty jaw tics. "The curse has a caveat banishing me. I can't set foot on Mākutu until it's lifted."

"And when it's lifted?"

Marcus shrugs. "I can go anywhere. Do anything."

"And that's what you want? To rule an island?"

"I want a *choice!*" He slams a fist against the apothecary cabinet he's leaning on, and one of the handles clatters to the floor. "I want to be who I am without having others' ideas of what that should be forced upon me!"

"And if I have to die for that to happen?"

"We all have to die, Kanu," my former lover shrugs. "It just happens more quickly for some of us."

"Fuck you, Marcus."

"You already did."

We stare at each other. All the things we said, felt, did, all the things we were, or could have been, bounce between us; two mirrors reflecting light back and forth until it turns to shadow.

"I don't want to force you, pet. But I will. Start the ceremony."

I want to protest, to resist. Demand my last phone call. But who would I call? Not Ari, she's probably catatonic by now. Auntie doesn't trust cellphones. Dean's a cunt, and my ex Bethany would have blocked me by the time she finished dousing her sheets in holy water to atone for the sins she happily performed on them with me.

I don't even have Bindi's number.

I'm alone at the end.

Like my mum.

Like my kuia.

Like my dad probably was.

Like we all are, I suppose. No matter how many bodies at the bedside, when your time comes, it's just you and whatever you believe in.

I believe in magic. Just like my ancestors did. That'll have to be enough.

So I start the ceremony.

Fi and I set most of it up before she left to perform her floral thievery. The crystals are in place, every piece of onyx, obsidian and black tourmaline in this place piled into mountain formations, interspersed with amethyst and clear quartz to magnify the absorption of negative energy. Some of the more potent ingredients from the back room – wood pigeon claws and marinated newt tails, both close enough to ingredients from home. Bowls of seawater and bentonite clay face their elemental homes, air and fire represented with incense and candles. I point to the top of the pentagram, the home of spirit, and Marcus steps into the space. The shadows seem to flex around him, stretching as if to make room for them both, the vampire and the man.

"Don't look so tense," Marcus advises me as I pour the salt and hyssop mixture around his feet. "You'll do great."

"The ginger's shit," I tell him. "We should wait for Fi."

His face darkens. "Now, Kanu."

"Kane."

"Kanu," he repeats, firmly. "You're working Mākutu magic. Use your Mākutu name for it."

"Bossy motherfucker," I mutter, but he ignores me. "Take your shirt off," I say louder.

"Why?"

"So I can stake you through the heart. Will you explode into ash, Buffy-style? Or is it more of a *Vampire Diaries* scenario where you bleed out?"

Marcus heaves a long-suffering sigh. "As far as I'm aware, it is ineffective. You would need to *Twilight* me."

"Dismemberment and *then* fire? I can work with that."

"Keep it in mind," he responds drily, unbuttoning his shirt. "If your ceremony is unsuccessful you may need it."

The sight of him standing topless in candlelight is a heady one and I'm struck by a sudden surge of empathy for all my fellow millennials who watched Skeet Ulrich lick corn syrup off his fingers and weren't immediately struck with disgusted horror.

Curse you, Billy Loomis.

The wind whips up the street outside, the glass in the storefront creaking behind the drawn blinds. "That's Tāwhirimātea, God of the winds," I inform Marcus. "He's saying you're a dickhead."

He remains silent as I arrange my own pounamu pendant at his feet along with sharp shards on onyx in the shape of a mouth. I arrange seagrass in a semi-circle and stand back.

"That's Hine-nui-te-pō, Queen of the Underworld," I tell him. "She said you're a dropnuts."

"Is this necessary?"

"Definitely. How can you expect the ceremony to work if you don't understand all the spirituality that goes into it?"

Finally, there's nothing left to do except start. I head back to the shop's small back kitchen where I *stupidly* left it to dry after washing it following our alley altercation. I flip it around and offer the handle to Marcus. "Cut yourself."

"You do it."

"Mate, you don't want me anywhere near your chest with a knife right now. The gods have nothing on the commentary I'd like to carve into your chest."

"Have at it."

"Stop fucking about. Take the knife and slice up a piece."

"Kanu," he glares at me. "This is blood magic. You need to do it properly."

"Well, excuse me. Some of us aren't as thrilled as you pretended to be about rushing to our own deaths."

"What makes you think I was pretending?"

"What?"

"Take what you need, Kanu. I'd hate for Fi to come back and open the door enough for your wind god to tell me I'm no good to my face. Might mess up the candles."

I'd hate for Fi to come back and find a vampire without a conscience in her shop. I don't know what her situation with Mira and Bash is, but Ari's call has convinced me that an un-cursed Marcus is a whole other beast.

I think for a second, and then flip the knife again, catching it by the hilt. It's freshly sharpened after this morning's activities, thanks to a sharpening stone Fi had in the back, so it slices through the skin of his pectoral like hot butter.

Marcus hisses, throwing his head back as I curve the first letter.

"Oh, sorry," I say, all faux-sweetness. "Did you forget the blade was silver?"

"I didn't forget," he grits out. "I just didn't realise you wanted to recreate a whole Jackson Pollock on my chest."

"Magic and art are symbiotic, Marcus," I intone solemnly. "I'm surprised you're not taking this more seriously."

He lets loose a hitching laugh as I start on my second letter. "Humans think we vampires are cruel. But we have nothing on your species for hurting others and calling it entertainment."

"Are you *not* entertained?"

"I am tired of this charade. Do the damn ceremony, Kanu! Don't make me compel you!"

"Fine." I pull the knife away from his chest and spray it with moonwater, saging it afterwards. "It'll have to do. Come on then." I draw the tip up my inner forearm, a thin ribbon of blood springing up. It hurts like a bitch, and I feel a moment of pity for the half-word I've opened on Marcus's chest until I remember I die at the end of all this.

Should have picked Supercalifragilisticexpialidocious.

But the Fi thing is a legitimate concern, so I dab at my wound with a thin swab of clean cotton and throw Marcus one to do the same. He tosses it back to me, and I wrap both pieces around a bundle of sage, chuck it in a metal bowl filled with more of the salt and hyssop mix, and set the whole thing on fire. I place it at his feet, letting the smoke rise up and curl around him. His jaw clenches as it reaches his chest, but he keeps his eyes on me.

Here we go.

I have to drag my gaze away to read the words chicken scratched into one of Fi's notebooks. If I *do* survive this, I'm going to owe her a fortune for the merch we're using. I take it slow, sounding out each new incantation in my head before I say it out loud. I practiced earlier, but fucking up magic with poor pronunciation isn't unheard of, and I haven't had much opportunity to use my native language for the past few years. I work through the text slowly, one time, then a second. At the end of the third I hesitate. Waiting.

"I don't understand," I say in English, looking at Marcus. "It should have–"

Everything goes black.

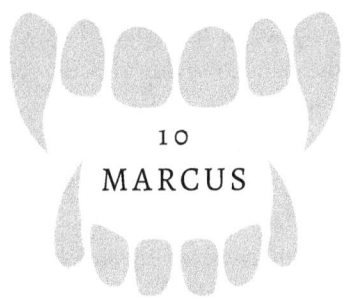

10

MARCUS

I roll to my side, trying to breathe. The smoke catches in my throat, clawing its way down into my lungs, choking me.

Breathe. I need to breathe.

It's a myth that vampires don't need oxygen. We're undead, not inhuman. Everything on Earth needs oxygen to survive. Replace water with blood, and we're basically sunflowers in a skin suit. Regular drinks, regular air, regular stretching routines, we need it all. Especially the stretching. We might not age at the speed of regular humans, but all those years before ergonomic seating really catch up after a few decades.

And that's not even considering the unexpectedly athletic sex I had last night.

"Kanu," I gasp past the rawness in my throat. "Kanu!"

"Fucking hell," a voice growls, and then I'm being hoisted by strong arms, pulled out of the smoke and laid across a velvet couch. "Take care of this one, babe."

"Kanu," I try again, reaching out but someone slaps a

blood bag into my hand. "Drink this. I had it in my purse, so it's warm."

I tear the pouch open and gulp it down. Excess blood streams down the outside of my mouth, spilling down my chin and onto my chest. I go to scoop some up with my fingers and pain shoots through me like lightning.

"What the hell?" Kanu's letters, carved into my chest. I didn't even watch as he did them, too focused on getting through the ceremony and making sure he didn't run. I look down. Is that a C? O? An upside down M? Was he writing something rude on me? Comebucket? I've heard young groups of idiots use that term before in a derogatory way.

It doesn't matter, of course. It'll heal. But I am curious.

"What the fuck, you lunatic?" Mira drops down beside me on the couch. "We leave you guys alone for a couple of hours and you summon the deep magic and almost burn the place down? Fire safety, motherfuckers. Look it up." She swigs directly from a brandy bottle and hands it to me. I tag one swig for comfort, another for courage, then pour a healthy dose over my lacerated chest.

"Ah, fuck that hurts!"

"That was badass, Deadbeat. Unnecessary, but badass." Mira nods back towards the main part of the store. "Fi's got the healing station set up over there."

Oh for Christ's sake.

I heave myself off the couch, glaring at Mira, who gives me a little finger wave. Fi and Sebastian are huddled together around a figure on the floor. As I watch, Fi starts chest compressions.

Kanu.

I'm by his side in a flash. "What's wrong? Why isn't he waking up?"

"It's alright," Sebastian says in that soothing low voice people use when things are certainly not alright. "As far as we can tell, you both fainted as a result of the ceremony. That was to be expected, but one of you knocked the sage bowl and the cotton parcel fell out, meaning the salt wasn't able to smother the flame. The seagrass caught fire. We put it out, but both of you seem to have suffered smoke inhalation."

Fi tilts Kanu's head and mouth, breathing into his mouth twice.

"Let me do it," I beg, fear and guilt rising in me like twin flames.

"You can't," Sebastian says gently. "Our breath doesn't work that way anymore."

Right. Fuck. I know that. We need it but we can't pass it to others in the same way.

"Let me... let me do the compressions then," I beg.

Sebastian shakes his head slowly. "Not that either, Marcus. You're too strong. You could crush his sternum."

I sit back, nothing to do but watch as Fi continues CPR. She mutters something to Sebastian as she counts and he digs into the floral embroidered bag between them and comes up with a small amber glass bottle.

"Three drops," Fi grunts, sweat beading on her forehead, "on each of the chakras."

Sebastian hurries to obey, starting by Kanu's feet, and Fi tips his head up again to breathe into his slack jaw.

Nothing happens.

"Nothing's happening," I say, my voice tight. "If I just–"

"Shut up," Fi snaps, her voice as hard as I've ever heard. "You've done enough."

I bite my lip, my own blood filling my mouth as I digest the truth of her statement.

None of this would be happening if it wasn't for me.

The temptation to turn and run is excruciating. I can't though. Not now that I've got somebody to stay for.

And then, like a miracle, like *magic*, Kanu splutters a hoarse cough.

"Kanu," I gasp, moving closer. Fi bats me away with surprising strength for a human of her age, and turns Kanu sideways. Just in time, the vomit starts only moments after, tears and blackened snot running down my pet's pretty face as his body jerks in truncated spasms, trying to rid itself of the toxicity.

"Give him some air," Sebastian murmurs in my ear. "He needs a couple of minutes to come right. Trust that Fi knows what she's doing."

So I wait, long tortuous minutes while Kanu's breath steadies, while he sips down water (still, I check to make sure) and allows Fi to check him over. Finally she meets my gaze over his shoulder and rolls her eyes.

"Okay, loverboy. Come say hola."

My speed is somewhat impacted by the rigours of the ceremony, but I'm still by his side faster than any human could be.

"Hello."

He squints up at me suspiciously. "I'm alive."

"Thank Heavens."

"So are you."

"Thanks to your gods too. Even the one that called me a dickhead."

"Is the curse lifted?"

I run my mind back to earlier, to the men who attacked Kanu and I in the alley. I don't feel guilty, though I didn't at the time either.

"Fi, lemon balm tea is atrocious."

"You're a snob," she replies easily, already investigating the ceremony site.

"I think," I say slowly, "the only way to truly know for sure is to return to Mākutu."

His cough-pinked cheeks pale. "You can't go back to Mākutu."

"Why not?"

"I'm not going to let you enslave my people!"

"Kanu. Kane." I cup his face in my hands. "That hasn't been my intention for a hundred years. Why would you think that?"

"Why else would you be so desperate to go back?"

I blink at him slowly. Does he really not know? He, who grew up surrounded by its majesty, its beauty? "I wish to retire there."

"What?"

"I wish to spend the rest of my days, however long they may be, in Mākutu. If the people will have me, of course. I understand there may be some hesitancy surrounding my residence, but I am willing to negotiate a generous settlement and strict terms regarding my behaviour."

"You… you said you wanted me to kill you."

"Yes. If we failed to break the curse, if that dream was shattered, then that was the next best thing. I did not want your fears for your people and your land to interfere with your ability to perform your magic," I explain. "I am sorry for deceiving you in that regard."

"But you were trying to kill me!"

I rear back. "I beg your pardon?"

"On the phone, Ari said…" he trails off.

"I would not be surprised," I offer gently after a few moments silence, "if my history with your people has created a prejudice against me based on my actions as a younger man. Nor would I be offended. That would be a natural reaction from a community that relies on each other for safety and support. But I have changed, due in large part to the curse your people placed on me. My goal, as I said before we started the ceremony, was to break the curse so I could have *choice*. Freedom to make my decisions and prove to myself, Mākutu, and anyone else that I have changed. Not because I *have* to through witchcraft, but because I *choose* to."

"Oh."

I clear my throat. "It would be an honor if, when you are feeling better, you would agree to escort me back. I would like to see it as it is now, through your eyes."

"You still want to spend time with me. Even now the curse is gone?"

Sometimes I do worry about the way in which indigenous knowledge can be lost between generations. Silly of me, they've survived long enough without involvement from outsiders, but this was common knowledge on the island a century ago.

"The curse is gone, Kanu. But the blood bond remains. We are fated to be, you and I. No magic can replicate that."

"Well, fuck," Kane rolls his head against my shoulder, and I press a kiss to his smoke-scented hair. "I have some phone calls to make."

EPILOGUE

KANE

Everybody wonders what happens when you die.

Not me. I know.

I know about the light on the other side, the way it beckons you forth. I know about the temptation, the sweet ache that pulls in your chest and whispers how nice it would be. To relax. To escape. To experience paradise.

I don't know if paradise really does await on the other side of that light, because I turned around and walked back into the darkness where my true love was waiting.

It's been two years since we broke the curse that my ancestors placed on Marcus. He still has a conscience, we've decided, but it's organic now. Homegrown. No more hundred-year-old dictates about what was appropriate and past mistakes tearing him up on the inside over and over again. He still feels bad about the harm he caused as a young vamp, but retirement has given him the luxury of time to seek out the families of those he wronged and make reparations where he can. He's anonymously donated school fees and sports trip costs, right up to affordable housing and new cars.

When Marcus said he wanted to retire, I had no idea of his concept of work. For a hundred and fifty years he'd been investing in the stock market, startup companies, a variety of industries. He even played professional poker in the 1980s.

The result? A vampire billionaire.

"What the fuck?!" Mira exploded when she found out. "Babe, we should off your dad!"

"Babe! No! Not cool!"

"That's my *husband*, you lunatic."

With Bash and Mira's help and significant input from me regarding Eternal Life Assurance *which it turned out he had a controlling stake in*, we've managed to swiftly drop Marcus's net worth to the high millions, and we're working hard on reducing it further.

One of his major investments? The revitalisation of rongoā on the island. We returned to Mākutu soon after our Vegas wedding (which he hated) and honeymoon during the Alaskan winter (which he loved as it gave him plenty of sun-free time before moving to a tropical island). The transition to Mākutu wasn't the easiest, but Marcus answered everyone's questions as honestly as possible and has continued to extend an open invitation to our place on the first full moon of each month so people can see him for who he really is – usually bouncing a baby on one knee, and showing the older kids how he can extend and retract his fangs.

I've taken up my kuia's position as the island's healer, but thanks to Marcus's funding, there are three new apprentices training under me so we never have to worry again about the knowledge being lost.

"Kane, pet? Have you seen the ceremonial carving knife?"

"In the shower," I call back, stirring my latest batch of ginger syrup on the woodstove. It's bright golden colour is testament to the replanting efforts that have meant the Mākutu ginger industry, and local families, are thriving.

"Why was it next to the shower?" Marcus wanders in, shirt off, fangs out. Perfectly relaxed and unbearably desirable.

My carvings faded from his chest within the month, and while my aborted attempt at labelling him a coward that fateful day stung to look at over the weeks it healed, I now sometimes scroll through my phone and look at the pictures we took in our early days together, the word COW scrawled pink and tender across his chest.

"Sexy times on Tuesday," I remind him, pressing a kiss against his lips. "Try this." I lift the spoon to his lips and he licks it clean, eyebrows quirking in clear admiration. It's a look I've grown accustomed to seeing on his face – he looks at me the same way whether I'm harvesting my own mānuka honey, giving a presentation on indigenous medicine at a major international college, or riding him with all the vigour of a college athlete.

"Decadent," her purrs now, wrapping one big arm around my waist and pulling me close. Our bare chests press together and I sigh happily into his kiss, the scrape of his fangs against my lips an erotic charge that has my dick thickening in my swim shorts.

"It was for celebration cocktails tonight," I murmur against his full lips. "But I could be tempted to use it for nefarious purposes instead."

"Nefarious, you say?" Marcus nibbles his way down my neck, burying his nose in the crook and inhaling. "I suspect I'd be easily persuaded."

I grind our hips together. "Big night tonight."

"Yes. Any nerves?" Marcus removes the pot and spoon from my hands, placing them down beside us. On a pot stand, obviously. Because that is a thing the Grovesnor-Tauhoes have.

I shake my head as he reaches down and frees my dick

from my shorts, the second snap of elastic signaling that he's there as well. And then he's spitting into his other hand and gripping us both, the slip slide of our dicks against each other in his wide grip made sweeter by the tingling numbness his natural lubricant provides. I jerk my hips harder, wrapping one hand around the back of his neck so I can look him in those gorgeous golden-brown eyes when I say, "No nerves. None, whatsoever."

The decision to get turned has been a big one, years in the making. Marcus has never put any pressure on me either way, but when I think about growing old and leaving him behind? A man who's already had to watch his family of origin pass on without him? It breaks my heart.

I've done a bit in my life. Seen some of the world, or the bits they say are worth seeing now. So has Marcus. But we haven't seen them together. So we figured, why not? My apprentices have a year or so left to go before they're qualified, and then we'll be off – a year long global adventure.

First stop to Apex City, to see Bash and Mira of course. Their unique approach to class warfare has the city looking a lot different to when Marcus and I first met there, and we can't wait to see the changes – aesthetic and social – for ourselves.

Tonight's the night of my transition, and after so long discussing it, I'm honestly just glad it's here.

"How could I resist you?" Marcus moans against my shoulder, nipping at me gently. I shiver and buck into his palm, the pressure of his own erection against mine skittering sensation down between my balls where I feel the telltale tightening. He drinks from me sometimes during sex, and I've grown to associate the prick of his fangs with an oncoming orgasm. "You were mine from the moment we met. Before that even. I spent a decade searching for you so I could spend eternity beside you."

"Marcus." I'm gripping him hard, one set of fingers buried in the soft dark locks at the back of his neck, the other clutching at one thrusting ass cheek, my grip so hard I'd leave bruises if he were human.

"Go on, pet," my vampire husband growls in my ear. "You know what I like." He suctions his mouth to my neck, light pulsing flutters of his tongue against my pulse. A moan rips through me. It's too good, too good, and then I'm coming. I sink my fingernails into the flesh of his ass, *hard*, and he bellows his own release, head falling back to herald it.

My turning was supposed to be romantic – silk sheets and champagne cocktails, under the stars of the Southern Cross.

In the end it takes place with us on cool kitchen tile, ragged and unchoreographed, covered in spunk, blood and ginger syrup, our laugher floating up into the island air.

It's messy.

Just like us.

THE END

I hope you've enjoyed BLEED THEM DRY. If you want to know about Bash and Mira, read their story EAT THE RICH by Elle Diaz.

GLOSSARY

- Kuia - grandmother
- Whakapapa - geneology, the ancestors and places that an individual or tribe connects with you
- Rongoā - traditional Maori medicine
- Rongoā Rakāu - traditional Maori medicinal plants
- Whenua - land
- Tāngata - people
- Kia ora - informal hello
- Mā te wā - informal goodbye - until we meet again
- Taonga - treasure
- Pounamu - New Zealand jade, commonly referred to in English as greenstone. It is a taonga, and traditionally should be gifted to the recipient rather than purchased for personal use.

ACKNOWLEDGMENTS

The biggest thank you to Elle Diaz for letting me jump on board the *Apex City Predators* sexy murder train when I got too excited helping her plan her book and couldn't help but want one of my own. Thank you also to Esme Brett and Cleo Browne, who expressed support from the beginning til the very final minutes of this very-final-minute submission because they always remember how bad my time management issues are before I do and continue in their genuine, but concerned, support. And most of all, thanks to my family (even the one that power-vomited down the hallway nine hours before this was due) and to you, my amazing and beloved reader! Thanks for taking a chance on *Bleed Them Dry*, and on me!

ABOUT THE AUTHOR

Award-winning author Courtney Clark Michaels has been reading and writing romance since she first pilfered a novel out of her mother's bedroom at the tender age of thirteen. Courtney's passion for writing strong, independent heroines and smart, sexy men is equal only to her passions for travel, online shopping and patting other people's dogs. She is lucky enough to live in the heart of New Zealand's winemaking region with her own opposites-attract hero, a few gorgeous children and a hyperactive poochon named Kevin.

ALSO BY
COURTNEY CLARK MICHAELS

PACIFIC PASSIONS NOVELS

Royally Screwed

Crown Chemistry

Heiress Undone

PACIFIC PASSIONS NOVELLAS

Ginger Kisses

Christmas In Paradise

Counting Down

Storm Warning

HOT RUGBY KNIGHTS

Game Changer

Off His Game

STANDALONES

Single Dad For The Runaway Bride

Also check out her selection of one-hour, one-handed reads under
her penname Tilly Otara!

Website

Insta

Facebook